He was really good at this—until he met her. Now he couldn't keep his head in the game...

A shark fight—he needed to fight to clear his head of how sweetly she responded to him in her dream state and how much he liked her taste.

Despite Lesia's words, Ainsley was not his destiny.

He slipped under the waves in search of his prey. It didn't take long. He missed the energy of spectators and the chants of protection.

Thoughts of Ainsley's soft lips and vanilla scent intruded.

The shark punctured his flesh before he could plunge his knife in for the kill.

He could use the portal to bridge time and space to get to the healers in one of the Alliance cities, but he would face sanctions from the Ruling Council.

Sea forms were only able to use the portal four times during an earth revolution, to prevent overuse and possible damage to the ancient oracle unless it was related to an ecommission.

It was easiest to pass through the portal from land to the depths during the summer and winter solstices and autumn and spring equinoxes. The summer solstice was a week away.

He would swim to land to heal there before he brought Ainsley back to the Crystal Caves to Micah.

Why did the thought of another male touching her make him angry? He swam quickly and felt the loss of his life force from his wound.

Gareth, a merman, will do anything to shark fight...

Even if it means entering the dreams of Ainsley Peters and making love to her so he can convince her to return with him under the tides to the Crystal Caves. Gareth faces sanctions and won't be able to shark fight unless he gets Ainsley, who thinks she is human, to see her grandfather. Problem is his love for Ainsley blindsides him. Can he convince her she is his destiny and he loves her more than shark fighting?

Ainsley longs to see her grandfather, but Gareth is asking more than she can give...

Ainsley Peters is afraid of the water. She thinks she's an ordinary elementary school teacher in Michigan. She can't forget the hot guy who shows up at her school. She has no idea the father she never knew was a merman. But then she dreams of Gareth—and he shows up in Hawaii where she is on vacation. He asks her to forsake everything she knows to follow him under the sea. Can she trust him with her heart and stay with him under the waves, the last place she wants to be?

KUDOS for *Restoring Ainsley*

"Eldana sweeps you away with an enchanted tale of mermaids, shark fighting, hot sex, and above all, love. You won't want to miss this mermaid story in *Restoring Ainsley*." ~ *Anne Lawson, romance author of Harbor of Love Series.*

"As with all of Eldana's book, this story is hot and sexy, with great characters and an intriguing plot." ~ *Taylor Jones, The Review Team of Taylor Jones & Regan Murphy*

"Eldana's character development is superb, and you can't help rooting for Ainsley. Heartwarming and sexy, *Restoring Ainsley* is one you won't want to miss." ~ *Regan Murphy, The Review Team of Taylor Jones & Regan Murphy*

Other Books by

Tara Eldana

and

Black Opal Books

Mer-Men Series

Under the Riptides

In the Depths

On Thin Ice

Other Books

Reclaiming Lexi

Double Dare

Cabin Fever

ACKNOWLEDGMENTS

Thanks to all at Black Opal Books who made *Restoring Ainsley* happen. Thanks to the Greater Detroit Romance Writers of America for the laughs, advice, and encouragement. And thanks to my family and friends for your encouragement and support.

Restoring
Ainsley

Tara Eldana

A Black Opal Books Publication

GENRE: STEAMY ROMANCE/PARANORMAL ROMANCE

This is a work of fiction. Names, places, characters and incidents are either the product of the author's imagination or are used fictitiously, and any resemblance to any actual persons, living or dead, businesses, organizations, events or locales is entirely coincidental. All trademarks, service marks, registered trademarks, and registered service marks are the property of their respective owners and are used herein for identification purposes only. The publisher does not have any control over or assume any responsibility for author or third-party websites or their contents.

DEDICATION

To all those who protect the integrity of our lakes and rivers and the life they sustain, and those who protect us from harm on those waters.

Chapter 1

Just do it," Sara said. "What have you got to lose?"

"Everything," Ainsley said.

It was the last week of school, and she was not on the permanent hire list. All the other teachers who were hired with her last year were offered tenure.

She was on probation for next year or until old man Hackett sacked her. She'd pissed him off when she'd asked for a different mentor, not knowing the asshole he'd assigned her to was his son-in-law.

Next week she would be leaving for Hawaii. Her Aunt Cathy had asked Ainsley to stay in her house on

Hawaii's Big Island while she went to Africa for four weeks.

The plane ticket from Michigan would blow through most of Ainsley's savings.

And vast expanses of water terrified her, despite growing up in Michigan, the mitten state surrounded by water. How would she stand being on an island?

She took a sip of the awful teacher's lounge coffee. "I could teach summer school, make extra money," she said. "It might help me get tenure, if they see I'm determined to quote, unquote, improve."

Sara put her hand on her arm. "Ains, are you sure you even want to teach?"

Ainsley recoiled.

"You're wonderful with kids," Sara said. "But you seem like a fish out of water. You had to start teaching a bunch of third graders two weeks after your mother died. You never shared that with Hackett, did you?"

"No," she said. "I was afraid he'd give my job to someone else, and I have my lease and student loans." She took another sip of coffee and winced. It was swill.

"Truth was you weren't ready." Sara lowered her voice. "I love you, sweets. But your heart isn't here."

Ainsley knew that.

But where was it?

"This coffee sucks," she said, in an attempt to change the subject.

Sara cringed.

Hackett stood behind her.

"Why don't you make a fresh pot, Ms. Peters? The pot is empty."

Ainsley twisted her mouth into a smile and stood up. "Happy to."

Not.

She put the filter in, switched the setting to strong, and flipped the switch to brew. How could he be pissed that she didn't like teacher's lounge coffee?

Who did?

Her only hope of keeping her job was if he retired.

Sara was right.

Ainsley should take a real break and figure out what she wanted to do, put her big girl pants on, face her fear of endless water, and go to Hawaii. She could spread her mother's ashes in the ocean like she'd wanted.

Cora, her mother, casually mentioned it to her over coffee a few weeks before a sudden stroke killed her at fifty.

Ainsley had never known her father. Cora said she had "joined with him," and she believed he had died at sea, because he never returned to her. She never said what "joined with" meant. Her mother got so sad whenever Ainsley asked about her father, so she stopped asking.

She'd only said her father's name was Reston, and he'd lived on a tiny island near American Samoa. Cora was a nurse, and she met him there when she went to help after a tidal wave devastated the island. Her mother never said what his last name was, and Ainsley had taken her mother's last name.

Her grandparents were a huge part of Ainsley's life until they'd died within a year of each other ten years ago. Aunt Cathy was the only family member she had left.

She sat back down, pulled out her Smart phone and credit card, and sent an email to her aunt saying she would come and got an immediate smiley face emoticon. Then she booked her plane ticket.

She lifted her hair off her neck, wishing she had put it up today. Sweat trickled down her back.

"I'm jealous," Sara said. "We're going out on the boat tonight. Why don't you come?"

Ainsley had never told her friend about her fear.

Sara and her husband Mike kept their speedboat in a harbor in the suburbs of Detroit. The other times they'd taken Ainsley out on Lake St. Clair, the stretch of water leading to the Detroit River, she could see the shoreline.

It could be good practice to get over her stupid fear of wide-open water.

"Sure," she said.

တၢတ

Sara's husband Mike started up the boat and eased away from the dock. It was a warm June night, and lots of boats were in the channel. Mike headed a different direction than he'd ever taken her before. She and Sara sipped margaritas.

Sara was telling a story about a kid who peed on a chair in Hackett's office, and Ainsley laughed so hard, tears ran down her cheeks.

The breeze turned brisker. Ainsley looked around and froze in terror.

Water. All she could see was water.

Her throat closed up, and the margarita seared her stomach. She struggled to breathe.

"Ains, what's wrong? Are you going to puke?"

"Shore," she sputtered. "Could we go back?"

Sara ran to Mike. He turned the boat around.

Sara took the drink out of Ainsley's hand, set it in a cup holder, and grabbed her hand.

"A panic attack, right? My sister gets them. What triggered it? I shouldn't have brought up Hackett."

"No land," Ainsley said as Mike steered back into the channel. "All water and no land, and I'm going to Hawaii. I can't do this. What was I thinking?"

"You have two weeks before you leave," Sara said. "I'll give you the name and number for my sister's therapist. Ains, if there's one thing I know about you, it's you can do anything you set your mind to. You'll do this if you want to."

"I'm sorry I ruined your night," Ainsley said as Mike pulled into their slip, and Sara hastened to help him.

"No problems, doll," Mike said. "Too many assholes out tonight, anyway."

Mike was a design engineer for General Motors. His tall, dark good looks were a perfect foil for her friend's pocket Venus curves and natural blonde hair. Sara rejoined her as he fiddled with the engine.

"Your husband is a dish," Ainsley said.

"I could fix you up. He's got a friend you'd like." Sara lowered her voice. "Punch that V-card, for the love of God. You must be the only girl who went to college without losing it to some frat boy."

"I was a commuter student working two jobs," Ainsley said. "Not much time for dating. And the guys I met were all jerk wads. Wasn't for lack of trying."

Mike looked up at Sara and winked. "Need a refill?"

Feeling like the proverbial third wheel, Ainsley told them she was going to drive home while it was still light out. She'd met them at the pier.

"Enjoy," she said, climbing out of the boat. Would she ever find a love like theirs?

ᶜᐣᶜᐣ

Gareth stood before the sea forms making up the Crystal Caves Ruling Council and scanned their faces for any sign they might go easy on him. He had ignored an urgent summons to return to the Crystal Caves. Work on the reef he'd been assigned to restore didn't take as long as expected. His ecomissions never did. The elders said he had a gift for restoration work and wanted him to take a leadership role, guiding others in the Alliance cities under the waves in that realm.

But Gareth's life force ran hot, and he used his spare time to shark fight. It was not sanctioned by the cities in the Alliance, but sea forms swam through the depths to watch the blood sport competitions. It was likened to bull fighting on land.

He was advancing in the rankings and had competed in the bout in the Golden Caverns before he returned here. He had been needed to restore a breeding habitat for whales damaged from a quake on the ocean's floor. He was always needed urgently somewhere.

But he deserved time for the blood sport he loved. It was the only time he felt alive.

He looked at Rylan, his fin mate, who held the ranking seat on the Ruling Council. Rylan had joined with Cari, a land form, and he had planted his seed inside her, again. She would bring forth their third offspring soon. Cari taught English language skills to sea forms still learning their fins.

Rylan's ruler face gave nothing away. "We have decided you will take time away from restoration," he said.

Gareth bowed and made to take his leave. He could still compete in the shark fight finals if he used his pass through a portal to bridge the vast distances between the cities.

"Wait," said Lesia, an elder member of the council. She was Rylan's mother's sister and had reared Rylan since his parents perished in the depths. She held out a quartz crystal. "You have been assigned a different task. Ovon wishes to know the female land form his son sired before he perished in the depths. You must bring her to him."

Ovon had damaged his fins on an ecomission and could not make long journeys through the depths, which were sometimes necessary if the portal was damaged.

Gareth stepped to the podium, looked into the clear quartz, and saw a woman with light-colored brown hair, with a reddish cast that fell past her shoulders, and blue eyes a shade similar to lapis lazuli. She had pleasing curves, and his cock twitched in response, but nothing more so than with the females who clamored to be with him after he bested a shark. The woman was on a mechanized machine that traveled over water. She struggled to breathe, and he felt an odd protective instinct stir to life.

The male steering the boat changed course. Gareth's land form language skills were not the best, but from the words he understood, he believed she told another female she felt fear when she couldn't see land.

"She is afraid of vast expanses of water and does not know she is sea form," Lesia said. "She will be at the place the land forms call Hawaii in fourteen earth rotations."

"It will be easier to bring her through the portal from there than from the lakes near her home, where she is now," Rylan said. "That is where Cari started her journey. She will help you with English before you leave."

Gareth looked into the crystals again and caught more words the female was speaking and grimaced. "She is not certain she can be in Hawaii because of her fear," he said.

Lesia's lips twitched in a slight smile. "Ainsley, her name is Ainsley," she said.

Gareth had fondness for the female who reared his fin mate. But what did she find humorous? He had no desire to go onto land, seek out this Ainsley, and bring her through the portal. "I would rather restore habitat," he said. "I'll take on extra work."

"You do not have a voice in this," Rylan said.

Gareth's life force ran hot.

How dare they?

He was best in the realm at habitat restoration, and he had agreed to resume his duties. He had no wish to bring a skittish female through the portal. "So this is punishment," he said.

Rylan frowned. The other members of the Ruling Council murmured among themselves.

Lesia stood. "I looked in the hall of records. This journey with Ainsley is your destiny."

Anger coursed through him. "No." His voiced rang through the great hall.

The Ruling Council stared. Sea forms did not raise their voices to the assembled ruling body.

But he could not accept this. He took a deep breath and struggled to speak in even tones. "I will not ignore a summons again. I will share my restoration skill with those in the cities in the Alliance, in a leadership role, if you wish."

He tried not to smile. They had been after him to work in a higher position for a time. This was perfect. He would be able to make time to shark fight in his travels to other cities when he was no longer under such scrutiny. He should have agreed to do this before.

Rylan stifled a laugh.

Did that mean he would support him in this?

"Gareth, we have decided," Lesia said.

He paced, trying to think. When Rylan joined with Cari, old Breton, now deposed, insisted that she must do so with free will. "Free will. I cannot do this because she must make the journey by free will."

"You must convince her or face sanctions for shark fighting," Rylan said. His voice was firm. "Ovon hopes she will join with Micah when she arrives."

Micah had charge of distribution channel for food to the Crystal Caves. Gareth found Micah's meticulous ways humorous. So Lesia did not mean that his own destiny was with this Ainsley, only that he make the journey with her. Relief rushed though him.

He felt no pressing need to join or produce offspring, unlike Rylan who had longed for Cari after seeing her in the crystals, long before she was born, and waited for her for another quarter of a century of earth revolutions. It was said that Rylan had joined with her in her dream state while she was still on land. Rylan's joy and happiness was apparent to all who made their home in the Crystal Caves. But, he, Gareth, had no such longings.

Lesia stepped down from the podium to where he stood. "You may have to, as land forms say, string her along, flirt with her, to gain her agreement."

That would be easy, and she would be Micah's to deal with after she arrived. And he would be off to his next reef and shark fight.

"Enter her dreams so she learns of you," Lesia said. "After she is here, you may take your leadership role and fight sharks."

He had one more thought. "Shouldn't Micah enter her dreams and bring her back?"

Rylan looked amused. "Micah could not rouse her from slumber," he said. "It must be you." Rylan's attention shifted. Gareth saw that Cari had entered the chamber. Rylan stepped down from the podium and made his way toward her.

Lesia patted Gareth's arm. Her face was set in stern lines. "It will be an adventure, not as shark fighting but the change will bring the excitement you crave."

Rylan claimed his mate and kissed her as if he was starved for her life force. Lesia followed his gaze and her expression softened.

Would Gareth ever feel such love for a female?

His mother and sire despaired he would ever join with a mate and bring forth offspring, although his sister Shara had given birth three times.

"Esteemed council." Gareth raised his voice so all could hear and he could bring matters out in the open. "If I bring this Ainsley back upon her will, and I assume a leadership role in guiding others in the Alliance in eco restoration, my shark fighting—"

Lesia clutched his shoulder. "This fighting puts you in peril. Your loved ones cringe in fear until you return.

They cannot bear to speak of it or watch the matches in the crystals. The Alliance cities tolerate this shark fighting—for now."

She hadn't said he would be sanctioned if he fought, merely scolded him for doing it. He bowed his head in thanks.

"Go," Lesia said. "Study Ainsley in the hall of crystals."

He had a better idea. He would go through the portal to her home near the great lake to ensure she made the journey to Hawaii. The sooner he started, the sooner he could get back to the only thing that made him feel alive—shark fighting.

Chapter 2

Ainsley took the last poster, a close up of a shark advertising *Shark Week* on the Discovery Channel, off her wall, rolled it up, and stuck it in a box. School had ended the day before. She hoisted her purse on her shoulder, picked up the heavy box, and hauled it out to the parking lot. She had to set the box down for a minute and stared at the school.

Why did she feel she would never be back? She'd had these kind of feelings before. They started in her gut. She couldn't shake the horrible feeling that she would lose her mother, who'd had no health issues that

Ainsley knew about before her stroke. Sometimes
Ainsley would wake up, knowing she would see a
friend that day that she hadn't heard from in a long
time.

For the past week, she couldn't shake the feeling
that she would meet a guy—the man of her dreams.
Except she didn't dream, ever. And she hadn't been on
a date on three months.

She bent down to pick up her box, hoping that
nobody else would come out and get a look at her ass in
the air.

"Need a hand?"

She whirled around. A guy she'd never seen before
flashed her a practiced smile and lifted the box off the
ground as if it weighed nothing. Their hands touched for
a second. Heat zinged up her arm like an electrical
current.

Holy hell.

He frowned. His hazel eyes looked stunned.

Had he felt it too? It was like they were joined by
live wires.

"Uh, yeah, thanks," she said.

His sandy brown hair fell nearly to his broad
shoulders.

Ainsley stood five feet, eight, and he stood a head
taller. He had a strong jaw and full, lower lip. He moved
like an athlete and looked like a movie star. He had to

have women falling over him. She watched the play of muscles under his T-shirt and admired his magnificent ass under his cargo shorts as she popped her trunk, and he stowed the box inside.

He saw the shark poster and whipped his head around, noticed her ogling his ass, and smirked.

He's *the* guy, her gut said—her brain…not so much.

No, he'd never graced the halls of Phillips Elementary before, that was for sure.

"I could ask you the same," she said.

He looked puzzled.

She smoothed her sweaty hands over her denim shorts. "You don't work here. Were you looking for somebody?"

There were only a few cars left in the lot. Sara had left an hour ago.

He flashed a phony, practiced smile again. She clicked her trunk shut. What was his deal? She was done with guys who thought they were God's gift to womankind. Derek had clinched that.

"You," he said.

"What for?" she said.

He smirked.

Seriously?

She turned away from him. "Well, thanks."

She got in her car and sped out of the lot. She had an appointment with Sara's sister's therapist.

છ૭ઉ૭

Gareth faced the Ruling Council again, determined to make them release him from his assignment to bring Ainsley to the Crystal Caves. Rylan laughed as the council peered through the crystals, watching him smile at her after he'd carried the box to her vehicle.

"She has no interest, and she will never agree to come here with me," Gareth said.

"You smile at her with disdain," Lesia said. "What did you expect, that she would offer herself to you as those do after you best a shark?"

"Micah should go," Gareth said. "Ovon hopes she will join with him. Micah is the logical choice."

Rylan's laugh sounded like the shriek of a dolphin. "Look at her face and your own when you touch her. And she has an interest in sharks."

Gareth looked into the crystals and saw his stunned expression when he'd brushed her soft skin. Ainsley's eyes went wide, and her full lips parted at his touch. And he'd felt the oddest compulsion to ensure she did not injure herself by lifting the box off the ground.

But when he saw her looking at him with interest and smiled at her, she'd recoiled.

"You look at her as if she were dolphin waste while you twist your lips into a travesty of a smile," Lesia said.

Ovon leaned forward "Was this blunder deliberate?"

Gareth narrowed his eyes. If he answered simply yes or no to the wily ruler, it would imply he was admitting that he blundered. "I do not believe it was a blunder. I wanted to begin as soon as possible to complete the mission and to spare her the anguish and fear of making the journey to Hawaii when she is afraid."

Ovon threw back his head and laughed. "I have known you before you learned your fins, since your mother brought you forth into this realm," he said. "Always you act in rash fashion unless you restore habitat. Think of my offspring's offspring as a sea form you would heal and tread with her as you would life forms you encounter on a mission. She is not a shark you aim to best."

Gareth gritted his teeth. He would miss an important shark fight unless he could slip away soon.

"Go to Hawaii and wait for her there," Lesia said. "Look in the crystals and see where she will reside and study her in the crystals before you leave."

Or he could get a head start, enter her dreams, journey to the shark fight, then to Hawaii after a quick

look in the crystals. He hid a smile. He could work this
to his advantage as he did in most matters. This served
him well in his restoration work, seeing the means to
the end. He bowed to the council, and they chanted
words of protection.

He set off for a quick stop in the hall of crystals,
making sure his shark fighting knife was sheathed
around his waist.

⁇

Ainsley kept the shade closed over the window
during the long flight over the Pacific. Her seat mate
was asleep. The therapist suggested she sit by the beach
by Lake Huron as much as she could before she left for
Hawaii.

So Ainsley rented a hotel room near Alpena, not far
from the lake, for three nights, and sat on the white sand
beach for as long as she could each day. She'd worked
up to three-hour stretches. She'd gotten a sunburn her
last day, skimping on sunscreen because it was an
overcast day, and her skin was peeling.

The therapist had asked her if she'd had a mishap
in the water as a child or if her mother had a fear of
water.

Ainsley had only swam in summer programs or at
her friend's family cottage on a small, inland lake where

you could see the shore. She'd only ventured onto the shores of the Great Lakes a few times with Derek and friends in college.

When she'd looked across the shimmering waters of Lake Huron and Lake Michigan, which seemed to stretch to infinity, tendrils of terror clamped around her heart. She would bury her face in a book or magazine, or play volleyball to avoid looking at the vast expanse of water and the tightness in her chest would ease a bit.

Had her mother been afraid?

She'd never said, but it made sense.

Ainsley would ask her Aunt Cathy. Her aunt was meeting her at the Honolulu airport. Her aunt's flight for the first part of her trip to Africa was leaving the day after tomorrow. Ainsley booked a hotel for one night. They would share a room and, after Aunt Cathy left, Ainsley would fly to her aunt's home on the Big Island.

ප∂පෘ

Her mother's ashes were secured in a small carry-on bag. The seat belt sign flashed and the pilots announced they were making their descent. They landed, and she opened the shade.

She blinked against the golden sunlight. She'd been travelling for ten hours, counting the two hour layover in Dallas. There was a six-hour time difference from Michigan.

The steward said it was eleven-thirty and eighty degrees. Ainsley felt dazed.

The feeling that she wouldn't be going back home to Michigan nudged her again. She pushed it aside. It was just her fear of the water, having to scatter her mother's ashes, and her crazy-ass dreams of late.

Every time she shut her eyes, she was with that guy in the parking lot.

She couldn't stop thinking about his mouth, his hands, the way he moved inside her, his hard body pressed against her—the way he made her come.

He was so not her type. He was cocky and arrogant, too much like Derek.

But every time she went to sleep, she dreamt of him—his hands on her skin, tweaking her nipples, his kiss and talking to him about sharks.

It was beyond weird. She'd never dreamed before.

She'd dated a swaggering jock in high school until he pressured her for sex. She'd said no. He'd dumped her and called her a cock tease.

She'd dated Derek for a year in college. He had dark hair and eyes, was tall, confident, and worked out a lot. She met him in the student health club and fell hard.

She was technically still a virgin, but not for lack of trying. They'd gotten each other off, and she offered to go on birth control, thinking he didn't like condoms, but he'd said no.

She found out he liked guys too when she stopped by his apartment to surprise him with some stuff she bought on sale at Lover's Lane. He'd opened the door, expecting a pizza delivery, not Ainsley in a trench coat wearing only a corset underneath. His guy waited naked on the couch.

He said he couldn't help it if both men and women were into him and asked her if she'd be interested in a three-some.

She said she wasn't and told him she'd wished he'd been honest with her. He'd just shrugged and swaggered back to his guy with a smirk.

She didn't judge him for his lifestyle, just his arrogance and deceit.

She got on birth control, determined to punch her V-card, but she hadn't met anyone who made her blood run hot until arrogant parking lot guy - not like she'd ever see him again in real life.

Pushing her thoughts aside, she stood up to wrestle her stuff from the overhead compartment and followed the herd off the plane to the baggage claim area where her aunt would meet her.

Her Aunt Cathy swooped her into her arms for a long hug. "Sweet girl," she said.

They hadn't seen each other since her mother's funeral. Aunt Cathy's boyfriend Rob hoisted Ainsley's luggage off the carousel before she could grab it, loaded it onto a cart, and put it into a cab. He was tall with a shaved head, bulky build, and friendly smile.

He rode with them to the hotel, got her luggage out of the cab, onto a hotel cart, and wheeled it onto the elevator then up to their room. His blue eyes crinkled into a smile. "You gals are on your own. I'll see you in the morning. Call if you need anything."

Ainsley stepped into the bathroom to give them some privacy. She came out when she heard the door snick shut.

Aunt Cathy's cheeks were flushed.

"He's nice, Auntie," Ainsley said.

"Yes, he is," Aunt Cathy said. "Would you like us to scatter Cora's ashes at sunset? A friend of Rob's has a place on the beach he said we were welcome to use."

"That would be good," Ainsley said, sinking down on the bed. She stretched out. She would shut her eyes for just a moment.

Her aunt shook her awake. An hour had passed. "I couldn't let you sleep any longer. We don't have much time together," her aunt said, looking nervous.

They had sandwiches in the hotel café then walked to the Waikiki beach, sat on a bench, and watched the surfers. Ainsley honed in on one guy. It was something about the way he moved. He reminded her of parking-lot, now-dream, guy. It must be jet lag, although she didn't feel sluggish.

Her aunt watched her closely." You're not scared of all this water?"

Ainsley watched dream guy ride the wave to shore then paddle out to sea again. "Not if I look at the surfers. I've been practicing sitting by the lakeshore near Alpena."

She took a long sip of bottled water. It was sweet that her aunt was so concerned about her.

Except, the only people she'd told about her fear were Sara and the therapist.

Ainsley clutched her aunt's hand. "How did you know, Auntie? I never said."

Aunt Cathy stared at the ocean and kept firm hold of her hand. "Ainsley, I have something to tell you. Let me finish, then I'll answer your questions. I wish we had more time before I have to leave you, but it will never be easy." She sounded so final and looked sad. "Cora thought she was doing the right thing when she made you afraid." Aunt Cathy shut her eyes and took a deep breath. "She kept your heritage a secret from you. Your father was of the sea. He told Cora he would come for her, and they would make their life under the sea together in a place with crystals. He never returned. She never knew why," she continued. "She was afraid if you spent time in large bodies of water, you would take your father's sea form."

Sea form?

"What's that?"

"Cora said he had a long tail and was human above the waist when he was in the water and a normal man on land."

Ainsley couldn't breathe. She turned her face so she couldn't see the ocean. Her heart thundered.

Her aunt pulled out her cell phone. "Rob, come now. We're on a bench on the hotel beach." Aunt Cathy, also a nurse, as Rob was, gathered her in her arms. "Breathe with me, sweet girl, just breathe."

When Rob arrived, he lifted Ainsley up in his arms. She chanced a look toward the waves.

Dream guy ran toward them. "She is not well?"

That voice—it was the same one she'd heard in the parking lot and in her dreams.

He looked more handsome than she remembered. Water glistened on his smooth, toned chest and that six-pack. He seemed angry that Rob held her." I am Gareth," he said.

"You're of the sea. You came for her, didn't you?" Aunt Cathy said, bristling with anger. "We're nurses, and we'll care for her until we leave. You'll have your chance. Cora said it must be free will."

What the hell did that mean?

Gareth nodded and stepped away. Rob carried Ainsley into the hotel. Her breath was coming easier. "Put me down, Rob, I can walk."

He did, but kept hold of her arm. Aunt Cathy took hold of her other arm until they got inside their room. They made her drink more water and lie down.

"Leave us for a bit, handsome?" Aunt Cathy said.

Rob enfolded her aunt in his arms, kissed the top of her head, and then let her go. "Later, 'k?" His love for her aunt showed in every line of his face.

"Always," her aunt said.

He clicked the door shut.

"Wow, Aunt Cath," she said. "He's the bomb."

Aunt Cathy giggled. "He is, isn't he? He convinced me to take this photo safari. It's geared to all levels from point and shooters like me to him. He takes wonderful pictures."

Her aunt picked up Ainsley's wrist, felt her pulse, and then touched her forehead. "Ainsley, no matter what surfer boy tells you, you don't have to do anything you don't want to do. Have you dreamt of him, dear?"

Ainsley nodded. She felt her cheeks flush.

Her aunt sighed. "It was the same for Cora. She dreamed of your father, very sexy dreams, before he showed up in the flesh when she was on that rescue mission. She stayed behind after her team left." Her aunt's voice broke with emotion. "Your grandparents and I went ballistic. She told us she fell in love with an oceanographer, and she was going to live off shore with him. Grandpa had his first heart attack then, and Cora went back to Michigan. She never saw your father again She waited and hoped. She didn't tell me what happened until after you were born. I had to give you your first bath. She was terrified—"

"I'd sprout a fish tail?" Ainsley laughed. "Hasn't happened yet."

"He, Gareth, didn't like Rob touching you," Aunt Cathy said. "He found us on the beach earlier. Somehow he knew I was connected to you."

"I saw him in Michigan at my school. He was a real jerk, like he knows he's God's gift to women."

Her aunt gave Ainsley the key to her house and car, told her about her neighborhood, and said to make sure she saw the volcano at night.

Ainsley asked her aunt for the name of a doctor. She forgot to get her birth control shot before she left. Her aunt wrote down a name and put it inside Ainsley's purse. "Tell the receptionist I referred you. You'll get in faster. In fact, I'll call and set it up now."

She made it for the day after tomorrow.

At sunset, Ainsley, Rob, and Aunt Cathy drove to Rob's friend's beachfront house and scattered her mother's ashes in the ocean. Ainsley and Aunt Cathy wept as the sun slipped under the horizon.

Chapter 3

Gareth watched Ainsley and her aunt weep. He stayed in his sea form in the shallows, fighting the oddest longing to hold Ainsley in his arms and comfort her. He knew from the crystals that land forms scattered ashes of loved ones in the sea for rites of death.

He never longed to hold a female for anything besides a brief joining where both went separate ways when it was over.

He'd wanted to haul her out the land form's arms and care for her himself. His feeling for this land form confused him.

She was a mission—nothing more, a sea form he had to restore to her true habitat.

A shark fight—he needed to fight to clear his head of how sweetly she responded to him in her dream state and how much he liked her taste.

Despite Lesia's words, Ainsley was not his destiny.

He slipped under the waves in search of his prey. It didn't take long. He missed the energy of spectators and the chants of protection.

Thoughts of Ainsley's soft lips and vanilla scent intruded.

The shark punctured his flesh before he could plunge his knife in for the kill.

He could use the portal to bridge time and space to get to the healers in one of the Alliance cities, but he would face sanctions from the Ruling Council.

Sea forms were only able to use the portal four times during an earth revolution, to prevent overuse and possible damage to the ancient oracle unless it was related to an ecommission.

It was easiest to pass through the portal from land to the depths during the summer and winter solstices and autumn and spring equinoxes. The summer solstice was a week away.

He would swim to land to heal there before he brought Ainsley back to the Crystal Caves to Micah. Why did the thought of another male touching her make him angry? He swam quickly and felt the loss of his life force from his wound.

He made it to the shallows and pulled a crystal out of his sheath to see where she was. He swam ashore through surfers to what the land forms called Kahului. He picked up a swatch of fabric the land forms used to wipe moisture off their skin, pressed it to his wound to stem the flow of his life force, then slipped his legs through clothing to cover his loincloth, and his feet into open flexible materials that covered the bottom of his feet and the top near his toes.

Ainsley, he wanted Ainsley.

℮ာ℮ာ

Aunt Cathy and Rob were flying out of the US from JFK Airport and spending a couple of days in the Big Apple, doing what her aunt described as cheesy tourist things.

They planned to Facetime on the burner phone Rob got for her after Ainsley got to Aunt Cathy's condo so her aunt could tell her where stuff was and how things worked. Ainsley made sure the phone was fully charged.

Aunt Cathy was supposed to call in twenty minutes. Her aunt had used the money she'd inherited from her parent's estate to buy the small condo and move to the

Big Island. Ainsley suspected her mother used her portion to help Ainsley with her college expenses.

Thud.

She jumped.

Someone or something was near her front door. She grabbed her phone and looked through the blinds over a long window next to the front door.

Holy hell. It was Gareth.

He held a towel to his bare chest and his shorts were falling off him.

She opened the door.

Her aunt's neighbor—a middle-aged lady with long gray hair with purple streaks—stood across the street on her porch.

"Is he okay?" She had a strong eastern seaboard accent.

Ainsley forced her shoulders, stiff with tension, to shrug. "He surfs," she said.

Purple hair nodded and turned away from them to tend her flowers.

There were brackets around his mouth she hadn't noticed before. "Come inside. What happened?"

He lowered himself onto the sofa. "Shark," he said.

She stood over him. Her phone chimed. It was Aunt Cathy. She accepted the call.

Her aunt's smile faded. Ainsley realized she could see Gareth behind her.

"I think he's hurt," she said. "He's got a towel stuck to his chest. It looks bloody. He said it was a shark."

"Fuck," Rob said. "Sweetheart, you need to cut the towel so it's only a bandage so you can see what you can of the gash without peeling the towel off."

"Scissors are in the knife stand on the kitchen counter," Aunt Cathy said.

Gareth shut his eyes and shuddered when she touched him. She pulled her hand back. "Did I hurt you?" she said.

He opened his eyes. The color gleamed like emeralds. "No, Ainsley."

She cut the towel away. From what she could see, the gash looked jagged.

"Hold the phone so we can see it," Aunt Cathy said.

"Is it bleeding?" Rob said.

Aunt Cathy worked on the floor with people admitted to the hospital while Rob worked in the emergency room.

Blood seeped from the towel.

"I think so," Ainsley said.

"Put pressure on it, Ainsley. Are you weak, Gareth?" her aunt shouted.

"Only fatigued," Gareth said.

Ainsley pressed against the towel as gently as she could. The oozing stopped.

"It could be infected," Aunt Cathy said. "He needs antibiotics."

Gareth's eyes roamed over Ainsley. She wore a cami top with a shelf bra and shorts. "Land form medicine will not help," he said. "I will heal, I have been gashed before."

"Watch him for fever and try to swab around the gash with alcohol as gently as you can. It will sting," her aunt said, biting her lip.

"He should get medical attention. Say he's indigent," Rob said. "This is fucked, sweetheart."

Gareth touched her bare shoulder. "Land form healers would put me and other sea forms in danger. May I rest? I will heal. I do so always."

"We're not leaving until tomorrow," Aunt Cathy said. "I'll call you before we leave. Crap. That will be three in the morning there."

"Yes, call me, Auntie." Ainsley ended the call.

Gareth needed clothes. He was sprawled across the couch. His eyes were shut. He looked paler than he did in the school parking lot.

Why was every moment of that burned into her brain? She couldn't close her eyes without seeing his smirk when he caught her ogling his ass.

She went into the spare bedroom, thinking Rob would have stuff there, even though he was much wider around the waist than Gareth. There were some shirts and pants in the closet, all too huge for Gareth.

In a dresser drawer she found some smaller sized cargo shorts and T-shirts.

Maybe Rob had a son?

She pulled out a pair of khaki cargo shorts and a black T-shirt and set them on the coffee table in the living room. Gareth didn't stir.

Her stomach growled. There was frozen pizza in the freezer so she started the oven and stared at Gareth.

He was so handsome.

What the fuck was he doing here, on her aunt's couch?

Why did she dream they were together, really together, every time she shut her eyes?

Her hormones were in overdrive.

As Sara said, she needed to get laid, pop her cherry, have no-strings sex, down and dirty, a quick fuck.

Why not take advantage of surfer guy or sea form, or whatever he was?

Ainsley snorted. Slim chance of that when he was recovering from blood loss and, for all intents and purposes, unconscious.

Plan B.

She would pick up some random hot guy.

Gareth had shown her in her dreams what she liked.

What was she waiting for?

She'd eat some frozen pizza then scope out a bar her aunt mentioned.

She'd pick up some condoms on her way. Starving, she ate four pieces of the pizza standing up over the sink then rummaged through her stuff for the sluttiest clothes she could find.

A short, blue sleeveless dress with a shelf bra she'd found on sale at Macy's with Sara, who'd insisted she buy it, called her name. Her friend said it made Ainsley's figure look like sin and her eyes amazing.

Ainsley shimmied into it and slipped on the one pair of black, stupid high-heeled shoes she'd packed. She went heavy on the eyeliner and red lipstick and put a flat iron through her hair to smooth out the waves.

She clomped across the kitchen floor in the heels and stopped at the sofa.

He hadn't moved. His color looked a bit better and the wound had stopped bleeding. She poured him a glass of water and set it on the coffee table.

Should she leave him a note?

What would she say?

Bringing some guy back for a quick fuck?

Could he even read English? He used such odd turns of phrase. She would tell random hookup guy the unconscious guy on her couch was her cousin, sleeping it off. She watched his chest rise and fall then squared her shoulders; grabbed the keys, her phone, and her clutch purse; and left Gareth, locking the door behind her.

ೕ೦ೕ

Something was wrong.

Gareth sat up.

His head was clear.

There was a glass of water on a low table. He felt thirsty and drank half of it. Land form clothes were there, too. He pulled them on.

Ainsley was not there. He knew that in every cell of his being. She'd left him alone in his weakened state.

Why did he care?

He was a shark fighter. He didn't need ministrations from females.

He pulled out the crystal to see if he could see her.

She was in a room with music.

A male was touching her.

Why did Gareth want to rip that male away from her?

Ainsley was not his twin flame or destiny, despite Lesia's words.

He would choose his own destiny.

He'd taken her in her dream state to lure her under

the waves—to restore her to her proper habitat, nothing more.

He heard engines draw near then stop, then Ainsley's laugh. She opened the door. A male followed her inside.

Gareth's jaw went slack.

He couldn't tear his eyes away from her.

She wore a blue gown that showed most of her long legs and clung to the swell of her breasts and buttocks. She'd used color on her face, red for her lips and dark brown around her eyes that looked like sky over land on a cloudless day.

His cock was hard as granite.

The male put his hands on her waist. Gareth took a step toward them.

"You were out cold," she said.

What was 'out cold'?

Gareth stared at the male's hands on her then at his face until he let her go and stepped away from her.

"You looking for a three-some, angel? 'Cos I'm down for that," the male said.

Gareth had watched landforms joining on films through the crystals and knew what a three-some was. He had no interest in males or sharing what was his with another male.

When did he start thinking that Ainsley was his?

She. Was. Not.

Her face twisted in fury. "No. I am not interested in a three-way." She pinched the bridge of her nose. "Seriously, another offer for a three-way?"

"I'm going to go," the male said.

He left, and she shut the door behind him then poured some brown colored water into two glasses and set them on the table.

She sank down onto the cushions he had rested on and shut her eyes.

Unable to stop himself, he sat beside her so their skin touched. She felt as soft and warm as he remembered. And she smelled like vanilla beans he'd smelled on islands he'd journeyed to for ecomissions.

He slid his fingers over her jawline and cheeks then into her hair. "This is different," he said.

She opened her eyes. They were darker, gray like water in a storm. "I straightened it. It waves, I hate the waves."

"It is so soft," he said.

She frowned. "Why did you chase that guy away? We weren't on the same page, but I didn't know that until you glared daggers at him."

Glared daggers? Nothing she said made sense to him. Damn his laziness during his land form language instruction.

His fingers rested on her arm. "You sought him out?"

She picked up her glass of liquid and took a small gulp. "Yes. I'm on vacation, and I want to hook up, nothing serious."

"Hook is sharp object that impales and captures small sea forms," he said. "You wished to capture that male to join with him?"

She stared at her glass. "If joining means what I think it does, yes. Hook up is slang for a fling or a casual relationship."

He remembered more from the films he'd watched through the crystals and her own thoughts came to him. *A quick fuck.*

He could read her thoughts?

Only twin flames could do this. It was essential to communicate in the depths.

He took a gulp of the brown liquid that tasted faintly sweet then set it down.

She was not his destiny.

So why did his life force run so hot at her intention of joining with that male?

He couldn't push the thought away that she was meant for him, only him, for the rest of her existence. It made no sense.

Maybe his head was his addled from his injury?

That would explain things. "So you wished to have a quick fuck to pierce your barrier?"

She spit out the brown liquid she'd been drinking.

"How did you know those words? I didn't say them."

Her thoughts came to him again. She wanted him to take her as he had in her dream state.

Her eyes were the color of tossing waves, and her pulse throbbed in her neck.

He ached to be inside her as he had in her sleep, hear the little noises she made when she became lost to her pleasure, and he hungered for her taste.

Seized by desire he had never known, he maneuvered them so she was underneath him.

He plundered her mouth, intoxicated by her taste, cupped her sex through the bit of material covering it, and grunted in satisfaction. He moved his finger to her slit.

She was wet for him. He ripped the material away from her skin, freed his cock, and rubbed it against her opening.

Her gown left her shoulders bare, and he pulled it down so her breasts were free. He lifted his mouth from her lips and nipped her shoulder then sucked hard on her neck, marking her as his.

He rose above her and entered her tight channel. "Ainsley," he said. "You desire to join with me?"

She locked her gaze with this and nodded. "But you need to use a condom."

He traced her lips, swollen from his kisses, with his thumb. "Sea forms do not carry disease."

"Oh." She lifted her hips in invitation.

He breached her barrier and stopped, allowing her tissues to stretch. Her eyes were a shade of turquoise. Her eyes showed her emotion. Would he ever learn what each shade meant?

He caressed her cheek. She pressed a kiss into his palm.

"You are happy," he said.

She sighed. "Yes."

He pumped into her, and she wrapped her legs around his waist. He tried to slow his movements, but she urged him to plunge deeper and faster. He thrust deep, bottoming out in her womb, and felt as if he had bested a shark to the roar of a crowd.

"Better than shark fights?" she smiled, reading his thoughts, then gasped. "How did I do that? It was like I heard you speak, but you didn't."

He pulled out and plunged deep, hitting the spongy part of her channel.

"Gareth."

She spasmed around him. He thrust faster and harder, rubbing her bundle of nerves until he brought her to pleasure again, raining nectar on his cock. He seized her hips and pumped into her, spilling his seed and felt her muscles contract around him.

Spent, he settled his weight over her for a moment before he withdrew. He found a cloth near the box she'd taken the brown liquid from, moistened it with water he saw her draw from a metal handle, and returned to her. He pressed the cloth to her sex, cleaned her, and glanced down at it when he drew it away. It was stained with blood from her first joining. He used his knife to cut a small swatch and put it in his sheath.

He felt a need to keep it.

She sat up and picked up her electronic device. He lifted her from the couch.

She laid her head on his shoulder and pointed to a hallway. "The bedroom's that way."

He set her down next to a large bed. She let her dress drop to the floor. He eased her onto the bed and stretched out. "We rest," he said. Exhaustion claimed him.

Chapter 4

Ainsley opened her eyes, feeling hot and sweaty.

Gareth had wrapped his arms around her, and he felt like a furnace.

Was that normal for his kind after they had sex?

She slipped out of his arms. He didn't stir.

Her cell phone pinged.

It was her aunt.

She slipped on her robe and answered the call.

Her aunt's face filled the screen. "How are things?"

"He's burning up, Auntie. He's sound asleep."

Rob's bald head came into view. "His pulse, can you find it?"

Ainsley took his wrist. "I'm no expert, but it's fast, like throbbing."

"Shit," Rob said. "You need to get him to an ER. His wound is infected. Baby, they're calling the flight."

"Rob, you go without me. I'm flying back," Aunt Cathy said.

"No," Ainsley said. "I'll take care of this."

"Ainsley, you have free will," Aunt Cathy said. "You must agree to what he asks."

"Last call, doll. What's it going to be?" Rob said.

"Go, Auntie, I've got this."

"I love you, baby," her aunt wept.

Ainsley wiped away her tears and smiled. "I love you, too, Auntie. Trip of a lifetime."

"For you, too, I think," her aunt said.

Aunt Cathy's face disappeared, and tightness settled into Ainsley's chest.

What did her aunt mean by this free will stuff?

She soaked a washcloth with cold water, wrung it out a bit, and ran it over his smooth, honed chest, then his sculpted jaw, damp forehead, and arms.

When had he taken off his T-shirt?

When he opened his eyes, she shook her head.

"You're burning up," she said. "I'm trying to cool you down, but you need a doctor."

He took off the sheath and loincloth and stood. "No. Land-form treatments will not work. Immersion. Is there a large receptacle I could fill with water?"

Forcing herself to look away, she pointed to the bathroom. "This way. I think you mean a bathtub."

Could he walk on his own? He followed her and waited as she filled the tub with cold water. "Get in," she said.

He fit his long body into the tub. She splashed water over the bit of towel stuck to his chest. It loosened, and she pressed her lips in a thin tight line. The gash was raised and red. She took off her robe, knelt by the side of the tub, poured liquid soap on her hand and, using the lightest touch she could, rubbed it over the gash.

He winced, reared up, took hold of her, and pulled her into the water.

"Stop, I'll hurt you," she said.

He set her between his legs so her head rested on his shoulder. She felt him harden and tried to move away. He pulled her against him and pinched her waist. "I must show you something," he said against her ear. "Restore you to your natural form."

Her legs tingled in the cold water.

She felt different. She glanced down.

"Holy hell," she shrieked.

Her legs were gone.

She had a tail, a beautiful tail in shades of blue and orange.

"This is your destiny, Ainsley. You are sea form, as your sire."

Bullshit. She wanted nothing from the man who deserted her and her mother when she needed him most.

"He left my mother," she said.

"He perished in the depths trying to reach her to bring her back," he said. "His sire grieves for him and longs to see you."

She tried to swallow the hard knot in her throat. She meant nothing to Gareth. He was only here to take her back. Well, she'd achieved her aim—a quick fuck, no strings attached. "You want me to go with you under the waves. No. Fucking. Way. Never. I'm afraid of large bodies of water."

She hauled herself out of the tub and stared at her tail, fascinated.

He snorted. "Is not your nature to be afraid. Who gave you this fear?"

She felt tingling below her waist. Her legs reappeared. "So you pinched me to make that happen. Can I do it myself?"

"No, not yet," he said.

She wrapped a towel around her and worked a brush through her tangled hair. He touched his wound and grimaced. Not. Her. Problem. "What is your day job under the waves when you're not fighting sharks?"

"I restore habitats. Many sea forms do this. They say I am best, and always I am called."

He smiled. Why did he have to be so freaking handsome?

"I am handsome freak?"

Fuck. She forgot he could do that—read her thoughts. "You are the best, so they sent you here for me."

"This is sanction. I ignore summons to restore reef to shark fight." He sounded tired. "You must return with me by free will."

So she was his punishment. This just got better and better.

He shut his eyes. Had he passed out?

Should she call 911 and leave him in their hands?

He'd said it wouldn't help.

He needed medical attention from his own kind.

She touched his shoulder. "Gareth? You need to go back to your home. You're ill."

He opened his eyes. "The volcano called Kohala. There is a portal there."

"I'll drive you,' she said.

He stood up and stepped out of the tub. She gave him a towel and took a flowered buttoned shirt out of the closet. "Put this on. It's so big, it shouldn't hurt your wound."

She found a pair of drawstring shorts. "These, too."

She pulled on her blue dress and slipped her feet into some flip-flops. He waited by the door.

She grabbed her purse and keys. Her aunt's compact had GPS, and she programmed Kohala volcano. It wasn't far.

ᔕᓂᔕᓂ

His gash throbbed. The healers would tend to it, but the Ruling Council would know he'd been shark fighting. And he would be returning without Ainsley. He stared at her profile as she steered the vehicle. She stirred something in his life force. He'd entered her dreams only to entice her to return with him to her true home, the Crystal Caves.

She was supposed to be merely a mission.

But her citrus taste, her vanilla smell, the way his cock slid inside her, the way she screamed his name when she rained her nectar on his cock—he couldn't let her go—most certainly not to Micah.

She was as essential to him as the essence of pure water.

How did this happen?

She would be furious with him for tricking her.

He would face further sanctions from the Ruling Council unless Ainsley said she was there, with him, by free will.

They drove to an area with other vehicles and land forms and stopped. She turned to him. "Do you know the way from here?" It was still dark. The sun hadn't jutted above the horizon yet.

He shut his eyes, feigning weakness, as if he was overcome with pain. She gripped his hand. "Come on, Gareth." She let go of his hand, got out of the vehicle, and came around to his side. She opened the door. "Get up," she said.

He stood slowly. More than one male looked at Ainsley. Her dress would get wet on their journey. He wished for her to keep it and wear it only for him. He put his arm around her, anchoring her to his side.

He would not let go. He could not let her go.

He longed to fasten his necklace, gemstones to match her blue eyes that would signify she belonged to him, around her neck before the journey, but he had not thought she would elicit such feelings.

He wanted to tell her that he wanted her by his side, that she was not just a mission, that he wanted to join with her, believed they were twin flames, but he feared she would not believe him. Why would she?

He found it hard to believe his feelings for her came so fast after joining with her.

The thought of another male touching her sent him into shark fighting mode. He steered her toward the path then through the brush to the portal.

"This way," he said.

He chanted words of protection.

"Is this it?" she said.

He took hold of her waist and pulled her into his arms and into the portal. He fused his mouth to hers, using the last vestiges of his strength, as they bridged time and space and stood on the outer ring of the Crystal Caves.

He lifted his mouth from hers and smiled. "You are home," he said before blackness claimed him.

ᥱᦔᥱᦔ

Ainsley, seething, sat on cushions in a room filled with natural formations of crystal that she guessed to be quartz.

She. Did. Not. Want. To. Be. There.

She should have guessed Gareth would use any means necessary to get her here to save his own, fine, magnificent ass.

She pushed thoughts of wanting him aside and fought back the waves of panic.

She was submerged under so much water.

Holding onto sea forms with fish tails, she'd swam through a channel to this room.

She hadn't sprouted her fish tail and none of them spoke English. Gareth had collapsed in her arms and was taken away. She hadn't seen him since.

Children wearing robes belted with sashes brought her a white robe with a gold sash and trays of shrimp, lobster, some sort of vegetables, and green grapes. They'd pointed at the mark Gareth made on her neck, giggled, and then left her.

She draped her wet dress over a bench and reluctantly slipped the white robe over her head. She didn't want the sea forms to see her naked but she didn't want them to think she wanted to stay here.

Famished, she started with the sweet grapes, moved on the succulent morsels of lobster and shrimp, then the crunchy vegetables.

"Ainsley? Can I come inside?"

It was a female voice. She even sounded Midwestern.

"Yes," Ainsley said.

A woman wearing a purple robe with a gold sash and slight belly bump appeared in the doorway. Her auburn hair was swept up in an elaborate style threaded with glittery blue crystals that matched her eyes. She wore a necklace of red stones that glowed like fire. She smiled. "I'm Cari from Grand Rapids, Michigan."

"Are they keeping you here, too?" Ainsley said.

Cari frowned. "No, sit down. Let's talk."

They sat on cushions next to a low table.

Ainsley noticed Cari's bare feet were wide. "I used to teach kindergarten," Cari said.

Waves of panic washed over Ainsley again. "Me, too, third grade. Are they abducting teachers?" She'd heard of Stockholm syndrome. Had Cari succumbed?

"I am here of my own free will," Cari said.

Those words again, free will.

"I am joined—er—married to Lord Rylan. He presides over the Ruling Council. We had a summit with rulers of the Alliance. My hair is usually down. Rylan likes it that way."

Cari's cheeks flamed red as the stones in her necklace.

Ainsley touched one of the stones. "It's beautiful," she said.

"They're real." Cari's lips curved into a smile. "It signifies I've joined with Rylan."

"Gareth, is he okay?" Ainsley said.

"The healers are tending his wound," Cari said. "If he had waited any longer—"

Ainsley shuddered. "He said land form medicine wouldn't help him. That's what I am, I guess, a land form." Ainsley's next words burst out in a sob. "I don't understand any of this. I'm terrified of large bodies of water and, apparently, I'm under the ocean. Where is this? Why am I here? How did I get here? He was supposed to be a quick f—fling, that's all."

Cari poured amber liquid into a goblet and brought it to her then wiped tears from her cheeks. "You are a sea form, like your sire—father—was," Cari said. "You didn't learn your fins, so you don't take your sea form unless your twin flame, husband, wills it."

What did twin flame mean?

"Gareth pinched me in the bathtub, and I felt all tingly then I had a tail." Ainsley's words came out in a rush. She sounded like a third grader. She took a long sip of the amber liquid. It tasted sweet and citrusy. "He said I was a mission because he was in trouble for shark fighting, and he would face sanctions if he didn't bring me back here. He tricked me," she said. "He kissed me and I forgot everything but him. I don't want to be here."

Cari raised her eyebrows. "He is still in trouble then," she said. "Will you at least meet your grandfather before you return? He longs to see you." Cari squeezed Ainsley's shoulder. "The portal was damaged by a quake on the ocean floor. Your father was swimming through the seas to bring your mother back here. He perished, died, on the journey. Rylan's parents also died in the seas from a torpedo during World War Two. Rylan's father was a land form, but shifted to sea form, like me. Otherwise, sea forms live long life spans and don't age like humans."

Ainsley pinched the bridge of her nose. "Holy hell." It was too much, all of this.

Would she ever see Gareth again if she left?

Did she want to?

"What did you mean Gareth is still in trouble?" Ainsley said.

Cari looked at her, a question in her eyes. "His mission was to bring you to us because you wanted to be here, of your own free will. You said you joined, had sex with him."

"I just wanted to punch my V-card," Ainsley said. Why was she revealing this?

"He was your first," Cari said. "You waited for him. Lesia, Rylan's aunt, told Gareth you were his destiny. He was furious. He didn't believe her. Did he offer you a necklace?"

Ainsley shook her head, remembering how Gareth got rid of the guy she brought home from the bar and the way he looked at her in her blue dress. "What will happen to him?"

Cari shrugged. "He will have lower rank and be assigned jobs where he will have no chance to shark fight. It's really not allowed, but the Ruling Council looks the other way unless it interferes with missions or bring danger to the Alliance cities. It's a popular sport. It's complicated."

"He would have lower rank?" Why did she care?

"He is a genius at habitat restoration, more skilled than anyone in the Alliance cities," Cari said. "He was going to be in charge of overseeing ecommissions as leader. He would have had time to shark fight."

"So he has groupies," Ainsley said.

Cari giggled.

That explained his cocky attitude the first time they met. "If I say I want to be here, will that let him off the hook?"

Cari drew a deep breath. "Yes, but he is still under the care of the healers, and he has memory loss. It happens to sea forms who get injured in the depths. Gareth lost part of his life force."

"He doesn't remember me," Ainsley guessed.

Cari sighed. "He remembers being assigned to bring you here. Sometimes the memories return."

So Ainsley could see her grandfather then leave all this water that terrified her.

No strings, a quick fuck, that's what she wanted, right?

Shit.

Her birth control shot. She missed it.

"Ainsley, you've gone so pale." Cari eased her over to the bed. "Lie down. I'll call the healers."

"I'm due for my birth control shot," Ainsley said. "Can they take care of that?"

Cari left the chamber and returned with two sea forms in green robes, a female with white fair and unlined face and a male with long white hair. Cari said words she didn't understand then turned to her. "Do you want me to stay? I understand if you want privacy. You need to take off your robe."

"Stay, please," Ainsley said. She sat up and pulled the robe over her head. The healers motioned for her to lie back down. They put different color crystals in a straight line starting in the center of her forehead and ended just under her bellybutton. "They're checking your chakras, Cari said.

"I thought all that stuff was bullshit," Ainsley said. "My mother was a nurse."

Cari laughed. "I know, right? My dad and brother are doctors. Medical knowledge here is more advanced. Gray, my brother, would shit a brick." She squeezed Ainsley's hand. "I didn't realize how much I missed using expressions nobody understands here."

"You miss Grand Rapids?" Ainsley said.

"I miss my brother and Jessie, his wife," Cari said. "She's a nurse. My sweet mother has Alzheimer's. We do something like Facetime. Sometimes she knows me, most times, not." She gripped Ainsley's hand. "But I love Rylan more than life."

Cari let her hand go, and the healers put their hands over Ainsley's heart, forehead, and pelvis.

The female handed Ainsley the robe. "There may be seed planted in womb, pregnant. Early to know for certain."

"Pregnant, I might be pregnant? From one time?"

The room whirled and everything went black.

Chapter 5

Gareth felt restless. Rylan said Ainsley was here in the Crystal Caves, and she'd agreed to see Ovon, her sire Rem's sire.

Gareth would not assume his position directing others in restoration work until the healers pronounced him fit. They thought rest would help the gap in his memory return.

Gareth felt annoyed. What need did he have to remember what happened during a few earth rotations?

His reputation as champion shark fighter was in question because he'd been injured in a shark fight. All sea forms in the Crystal Caves knew he had lost a fight.

Even though he had killed his opponent and took the tooth to prove it—technically he'd lost the fight.

Rylan and Cari invited him to a small feast in their private chambers. He, Ainsley, Ovon, and Micah—who'd made his intention to join with Ainsley—would dine together.

Why did the fact that Micah wished to join with Ainsley raise Gareth's fighter's instinct? He found Micah and his talk of his task of monitoring the endless details of food supply for the Crystal Caves to be as boring as language lessons.

But why did the thought of Micah and Ainsley together spark his anger?

Gareth stepped into Cari and Rylan's chamber. Rylan kissed Cari as though he was infusing her with his life force for a journey through the portal to bridge time and space.

Gareth chanted his thanks for their hospitality. Rylan grunted and released her, but kept her firmly anchored to his side. "The shark fighter has torn himself away from the females rejoicing he has returned," Rylan said.

Gareth frowned. He'd found the female's attentions annoying, which was usually not so. He'd casually joined with female sea forms after other shark fights, but felt no need for release with them now. Was he still healing?

"Come," Rylan said, switching to English. "Our guests await."

Gareth supposed courtesy dictated they speak Ainsley's language, although Cari was quite skilled in the language of the Crystal Caves and could easily translate for Ainsley.

Gareth's English words were not as good as other sea forms.

They entered an inner chamber where they would dine.

A female who must be Ainsley stood with her back to them, speaking to Ovon. Micah didn't take his adoring eyes from Ainsley.

Anger swept through Gareth's life force. Had he formed an attachment to this female he couldn't remember? He stepped toward her.

Ainsley turned to face them.

Gareth halted mid-step.

Her blue eyes reminded him of the sea under a cloudless sky. She wore her auburn hair in a braid over her shoulder.

Her neck was bare. She wore no necklace, and he stared at the beautiful lines of her neck. There was a mark on her skin. Had he put it there on the journey?

His cock hardened, and he stepped closer, compelled to be near her and touch her.

Gareth bowed to Ovon, nodded to Micah, and took

hold of her hand. A bolt of energy arced up his arm. Had she felt it, too?

Her eyes changed color to stormy gray. A memory surfaced—her eyes reflected her emotions. What did stormy gray mean?

He kept hold of her hand. "Ainsley, you are well?"

Ovon took Gareth's, then Ainsley's, full measure. Cari sipped from a crystal goblet and spoke with Micah, who launched into a long explanation of the procurement of sea urchin as Gareth drew closer to Ainsley. She smelled like vanilla beans and cinnamon sticks.

"Yes, Gareth," she said. He loved his name on her lips. Had he tasted them?

Her eyes took on a silvery cast. "And you," she said. "Are you healed? Do you remember your time on land?"

She sounded angry. His cock twitched. He was grateful his robe hid the bulge, although he wished he could adjust his loincloth.

A blue gown came to his mind. He didn't realize he'd said the words out loud.

Ainsley's eyes widened. "Yes, I wore a blue gown when you brought me here."

He frowned. The gown had showed her bare shoulders and legs. Another memory surfaced.

"Three-some," he said.

Cari choked on her drink, and Rylan took hold of her.

"A male said this and you grew angry," Gareth said.

Ainsley's cheeks flamed red.

Cari spoke softly to Rylan, who threw back his head and laughed until Cari jabbed her elbow into his ribs.

"The servers have everything ready," Cari said.

Rylan led them into a chamber filled with amethyst formations. Gareth held Ainsley's hand and followed. "The artisans did these for me," Cari said. "This is one of my favorite spaces in the Crystal Caves."

Rylan nuzzled Cari's neck above her ruby necklace, drew her down on cushions, and settled her between his legs. This was the custom for males in informal settings and in private chambers to see their female was fed the finest morsels of food before they took their own food.

Gareth maneuvered Ainsley on the cushions so they were touching. They bowed their heads in an ancient chant of thanks. Ainsley lowered her head, and Gareth draped his arm across her back and touched her shoulder, as if he had the right to do so. He longed to feel her skin under the fabric of her robe.

He selected a bite of lobster infused with savory sauce and, on instinct, brought it to Ainsley's lips.

She gasped, and he drew back, alarmed. "You are sickened by fish in a shell?" The healers said some land forms were afflicted with this.

"No," Ainsley said. "Why are you feeding me?"

His head throbbed. "I do not know," he said.

"He is remembering," Cari said.

Ainsley took his offering and moaned. "This is amazing," she said.

The sound she made aroused him further. His cock could pierce shark flesh.

He didn't feed her again but kept his arm around her shoulders, not knowing why.

e✍e✍

Ainsley tried to listen to Micah describe how he managed the supply chain. Micah's English was good, better than Gareth's, but she couldn't follow anything he said with Gareth touching her.

Why was he doing it?

Gareth turned his face into her neck and inhaled.

She dropped the bite of shrimp she had been holding.

Was this some custom under the sea? Inhaling someone's scent? Did she even have one?

She stared at the amethyst crystals. Faces of animals and people seemed to beckon her from inside the glittering facets of the purple formations. The longer she stared, the more faces she saw. It made her dizzy so she dropped her gaze.

Micah stopped speaking to drink from his goblet.

"The amethyst gives off a high vibration in the depths," Cari said. "Some are sensitive to it."

"I feel a little dizzy when I look at them," Ainsley said. "I see faces of animals and people."

Cari's hand covered the soft swell of her belly. "Really? You're the first to say that," Cari said. "I have to limit my time here when I'm pregnant because I get a buzz. The healers say it won't harm the baby, but I'm paranoid."

"When are you due?" Ainsley said.

"Three months land time," Cari said. "Gestation is shorter here. Childhood takes the same time span as on land but adulthood lasts a lot longer."

"Sea forms do not age as land forms," Rylan said.

"I have drawn breath for four hundred earth revolutions," Ovon said, chuckling.

Ainsley gasped and embraced Ovon. "I'm so happy I met you, Grandpa."

She broke away and squeezed his hand. How old had he been when her father was born? Had her grandmother died? Did she have aunts, uncles, or cousins? How many children did sea forms have if they lived so long?

Cari said some words in the language of the Crystal Caves. Ovon bent his head and chanted.

Rylan, Micah, and Gareth bowed their heads while Ovon chanted. Cari's eyes welled with tears. "I explained what Grandpa means," she whispered. "He chanted his thanks that you have accepted him as your kin and that you have come under the waves to be with him. He grieved so deeply for his mate, then his son. They both perished in the seas. You are his only family. He wanted to see you while he still drew breath. Four hundred is old for sea forms."

Sea forms. The sea.

She was under so much water.

Her chest tightened, and she struggled to breathe.

Ovon frowned.

Gareth turned toward her.

She couldn't speak. She could only stare into his impossibly green eyes. Rylan said words she couldn't understand.

Gareth lifted her in his arms and carried her out of the chamber—over what sounded like protests from Micah—through a winding passage to a large chamber and set her onto a bed...his bed?

"Oui, yes," he said.

Had she spoken out loud?

"Again, yes," he said. He smiled at her. "Your breath is coming better?

"Yes." As soon as he'd touched her, the panic evaporated.

"Rylan believes you had attack of panic. Cari also had water fear."

Water?

Her chest seized up again. Gareth sat next to her and held her hands.

She took deep breaths. "Large bodies of water terrify me. That's why I can't be here."

He looked confused. He let go of one of her hands and traced circles on her neck just below her ear before he spread his fingers over her throat. Heat shot to her core.

"You are here. Do words have other meaning? My English sucks."

Despite her panic, she giggled. "Sucks?"

He grinned and her heart flipped. "I hear it on TubeYou," he said.

"YouTube," she said. She wanted to press her lips to his palm, roughened by his work and shark fighting.

He was a shark fighter.

That came first for him. It was the only reason he came for her. She had to remember that.

He stared at her lips.

Talk, she had to talk.

"The words do have a different meaning," she said. "I don't want to stay someplace where I feel so afraid.

Thank-you for bringing me here to meet my grandfather. It's all good, right? For you, I mean?"

He traced circled on her nape and lifted his gaze to hers. "For me?"

His green eyes glittered with flecks of gold.

Why couldn't she pull away from him?

"You will get a better job so you can shark fight. I was a mission for you. You succeeded. You've got what you wanted."

He shut his eyes and traced her lips with his thumb. "I have memories. We joined on land. I was angry you were with that male. He saw you in your blue gown."

He trailed kisses from her ear toward her lips. She felt boneless. She was wet with wanting him.

"Ainsley, I smell your desire. You want me?"

She felt her cheeks flame and lowered her eyes.

He tilted her chin up so she had to look at him. "I was first to breach your barrier." He stood and shed his robe. "Why, Ainsley? You wait for me. I was your first male."

Faint scars dotted the golden skin of his broad, hairless chest.

Shark scars?

His loincloth hung low on his hips, just above his washboard abs.

She could see his cock bulge under the loincloth.

What if she carried his child?

Would he look at her the way Rylan looked at Cari, as if she was dearer to him than his own life? "I might be pregnant," she said. "The healers aren't sure."

His eyes gleamed gold. Was he angry?

He held his hand out to her, drawing her to her feet. He took hold of the edge of her robe and drew it over her head. Her nipples beaded for wanting him. He dropped to his knees and pressed her so her butt rested on the bed and lifted her legs over his shoulders. "I must taste you."

He pressed two fingers inside her and pressed his tongue to her clit. She dug her nails into his shoulders, piercing his skin. He didn't flinch. His tongue and fingers worked magic. She burst apart with the force of her orgasm and screamed his name. He rose over her, yanked off his loincloth, and entered her in one smooth stroke.

He fused his mouth to hers, and she tasted herself. He dragged his dick along her nerve endings then hit what must have been her G-spot and lifted his mouth from hers. He pinched her nipples and she came again.

"You are so tight," he said. His eyes glittered. "I had to be inside you, but will not spill my seed inside you unless you wish it."

"No, please don't," she said.

He pumped into her twice then pulled out, took his cock in his hands and came in hard spurts on her stomach, breasts, and neck. He pulled her up and kissed her again, pressing her against him so his cum coated his skin, too.

He broke away and took her hand and led her to another chamber with a pool of water that flowed into a channel. He took hold of her waist, pinched it, lowered her into the water, and dropped in beside her. His essence dissolved from her skin and she felt sad.

Her legs tingled. She squealed with joy as she took her sea form. Her tail was a mix of blues and oranges.

Gareth's sea form was a mix of green that matched his eyes and red.

"You must learn your fins," he said.

"But why do I only take sea form when you pinch my waist?" she said.

He frowned. "The sages say only twin flames have this power," he said.

Twin flames?

Was he angry?

"So you're saying you're the only one who can make me like this?"

"For now, until you learn your fins," he said flatly.

She wanted to ask what twin flame meant, but he seemed suddenly distant.

She would ask Cari or Ovon.

He kissed her again, an angry sort of kiss, and plunged them under water. He turned her so he had firm hold of her waist, and propelled her through the underwater darkness, through the channel.

She was breathing underwater.

ᏉᎦᏉᎦ

Gareth swam Ainsley through the channel to the Crystal Caves the city was named for.

He shouldn't have touched her, but his head got addled when she was near him and his cock took over. The thought that another male would touch her and claim her raised his shark-fighting instincts.

A shark fighter—that was what he was at the core of his being.

He was not meant to join with one female. She was not his twin flame.

He was skilled at habitat restoration. It must be this skill that enabled him to change her into sea form.

He was restoring Ainsley—that was all.

They surfaced. He pulled her onto a ledge and pinched her so she would take her land form.

She stared in awe at the formations of rose quartz and sugilite in the Caves.

He wished there were robes here they could cover themselves with. Looking at her made his cock hard as the crystal, and he didn't want another male to see her.

He swallowed hard. His possessiveness of her was

misplaced and unwelcomed. She did not want to stay here, and shark fighters did not have twin flames. She did not want his seed inside her.

He had to remember these things.

But what if she already carried his offspring?

That would change everything. Something softened inside him, and he felt settled and whole for the first time in his existence.

"Gareth?" It was his sire. Ainsley jumped behind him.

His parents came forward, smiling and holding white robes. Gareth took them and donned a robe before he turned, shielding Ainsley. He slipped the robe over her head. She slid her arms into the sleeves as he held her braid.

He turned to his parents.

His sire bowed his head. "I am Gareth's sire Enden."

"And I am his mother Salina. Welcome." She bowed to Ainsley and Ainsley repeated the gesture.

His mother drew Ainsley to her side. Gareth switched to the language of the Crystal Caves. "How did you find me, us?" Gareth asked.

Enden laughed. "This has been your favorite place since before learned your fins."

Ainsley laughed at his mother's words, drawing Gareth's gaze.

"Your mother rejoices you have found your twin flame and thinks you will stop fighting sharks," Enden said, staring hard at Gareth. "I see from your face that you still wish to fight."

Gareth shrugged. "She does not wish to stay. She has fear of open seas."

Enden put his hand on Gareth's shoulder. "But she may carry your offspring," he said.

Gareth stopped short. "How do you learn this?"

Enden looked at his mother.

Gareth should have realized they could keep no secrets in the Crystal Caves, especially from Salina, who could discover anything if she wished.

"You hope for this," Enden said, sounding surprised. "I see this, also."

"She must stay of her free will," Gareth said.

"Micah wishes to join with her," Enden said. "He has selected a necklace."

"No," Gareth said, loudly.

Ainsley stared.

Salina came to his side and lapsed into the language of the Crystal Caves. "Are you unwell?" She put her hand to his forehead. "The healers said your head could pain you when your memories return."

He chanted his thanks to Salina for her concern. "My memories returned," he said.

Enden took his wife's hand. "I told him Micah will ask Ainsley to join with him.'

Salina sighed. "He has no care if she carries your offspring. He wishes to love and care for her and your offspring, if you have planted your seed."

Gareth bristled.

Ainsley came to his side. She looked worried.

"I am sorry we do not use English words," Salina said.

Enden took hold of Ainsley's arm and Salina squeezed her hand.

"Let us show you the best part of this space," Salina said.

They led Ainsley away, leaving Gareth to trail behind.

His mother's words drew laughter from Ainsley. His parents felt tenderness and affection for her. Enden and Ainsley's sire learned their fins together.

Chapter 6

Gareth's head throbbed. Another memory surfaced. After he joined with Ainsley and breached her barrier, he had planned to claim her before he brought her to the Crystal Caves. He'd wanted to fasten a sapphire necklace to match her eyes around her throat to keep the other males, and those who would hate her, at bay.

Some sea forms hated land forms because they blamed them for fouling the land and water. Cari still faced prejudice and hate from sea forms because, although she was a shifter, she had been born wholly land form.

Rylan had looked into the crystals a hundred earth revolutions ago and seen her long before she was born. He waited for another quarter century to claim her for his queen.

How had Rylan been so sure? Rylan had nearly given up his destiny to rule the Crystal Caves for Cari.

Gareth was different.

Shark fighting was as essential to him as the pure essence of water. It balanced the focus, care, and detail he needed to restore damaged eco systems in the depths and shallows.

Shark fighting was in his life force.

But as he watched Ainsley with Endon and Salina, he felt Ainsley was as much a part of him as shark fighting.

How could he step away from her and watch her make a life with Micah, if she decided to stay? How could he let her leave and make her life on land, away from him?

Could she join with Gareth in the depths, someone who had lust for the kill?

He caught up with Ainsley as his mother stared into a quartz crystal she held in her hand.

Salina gave the crystal to Gareth. "The healers, they send a message."

Ainsley did not carry his offspring.

That was it, then.

She could stay if she wished, but he had no tie to her.

It was simple.

Except it wasn't.

Why did he feel like his life force was seeping away from him?

"We'll leave you, now," Salina said.

Ainsley smiled at his parents. "It was so nice to meet you."

Endon looked at Gareth, spoke words in the language of the Crystal Caves, then took Salina's arm, and drew her away.

Ainsley gripped Gareth's arm. Her face looked strained. "Is everything okay? You seem upset."

Her eyes were blue like the sapphires he wanted to fasten around her neck. "You do not carry my offspring," he said. "The healers are certain. Message came through the crystal."

Her hand strayed to her belly.

"Oh," she said. "What did your father say?"

He dropped his gaze. "That Micah wants to join with you."

"You mean marry me, like Cari and Rylan and your parents?"

"Yes, be husband to you. You must stay by free will."

She took hold of his hands. He looked at her heart-shaped face and soft, pink lips. "What do you want, besides shark fighting?" she said.

He pulled her closer to him. Her, he wanted her.

"Gareth?" Salina's voice called out. "Ainsley's kin, sister to Cora, her life force ebbs. Lesia saw this in the hall of crystals."

"Aunt Cathy? She walks a mile a day and takes yoga classes twice a week."

Gareth took Ainsley's hand and guided her through the passageways to the hall of crystal.

※※※

Had her aunt injured herself or fallen ill in Africa? What if, anything could Ainsley learn by looking through quartz?

Cari and a dark-haired woman stood next to a pillar of quartz in the center of the hall. Ainsley clutched Gareth's hand.

"This is Lesia," Cari said. Lesia dipped her head, smiled at Ainsley, and glanced at her hand clasped in Gareth's.

Ainsley stared doubtfully into the crystal. She saw cloudy images that became clearer, but the sound wasn't in sync with the images.

Aunt Cathy was in a bed and Rob sat next to her. "I'm sorry we had to cut the vacation short," Aunt Cathy said.

Where were they?

"Oahu, Queen's Medical Center," Cari said.

Ainsley didn't realize she'd spoken out loud.

"I've been watching," Cari said.

"Good thing. Your color was terrible and you were so tired," Rob said. "A bypass is not something you have where you don't speak the language," he said.

"Did they say what time?" Aunt Cathy said.

"Today, they're not sure when," Rob said. "That's why you can't eat. Fucking surgeons."

The images grew so blurry she couldn't see anything.

Tears streamed down Ainsley's cheeks. "I need to be with her," she said.

Cari looked at Gareth. He nodded.

Ainsley realized she'd been holding his hand in a death grip and let it go.

Ovon, Gareth's parents, and Rylan came toward them. "You leave us," Ovon said.

Ainsley could only nod, too overcome with emotion to speak. She hugged him and, after Cari said words she didn't understand, Ovon hugged her back.

"The portal, Ainsley, is easiest if we leave now," Gareth said.

We?

He was coming with her?

Rylan's lips quirked into a smile. Gareth took a knife and sheath from his father and turned away from them to secure it under his robe. His father also handed him a sapphire necklace, which he also secured, which puzzled her. Before she could ask about it, Ovon lowered his head and chanted and the others joined in.

"Words of protection," Gareth said.

"Goodbye, Ainsley," Cari said, hugging her.

"Thank you, Cari, for everything." Ainsley stepped away as Rylan took hold of Cari's waist and pulled her back against him.

Ainsley followed Gareth through a series of winding corridors. He stopped at a shadowy corner, shrugged out of his robe, pulled her robe over her head, then pulled her into his arms.

He pressed his lips to hers. She opened her mouth for him and was lost to his kiss. He lifted her so her breasts pressed into his rock hard chest, and his erection nudged against her sex.

He pinched her waist and they were pulled into a vortex—into water and darkness.

She felt her sea form and Gareth's firm hands gripping her waist.

His thoughts came to her.

We must swim for shore. I will never let you go.

Never?

She tried to match his movements.

He gripped her waist. *You are learning your fins.*

How much longer till they reached shore? She was swimming through so much water—the endless Pacific. So much water. Her chest seized with panic.

He kissed her again, and her panic dissolved. He propelled them through the water. A deep, melodic voice crooned a song in her head that reminded her of a child's lullaby.

Was Gareth singing?

She could see light in the water. Were they coming to shore?

They were naked.

Holy hell.

Gareth pushed her head out of the water. It was midday. The sun was straight overhead. The beach was packed and everyone was nude.

It was a nude beach. She giggled then remembered she still had her sea form. She turned to Gareth, swirling her tail around him.

He scanned the shore and pointed to a spot past the nude sunbathers. "Go there to dry out so you take land form."

He didn't touch her, so she propelled herself through the shallows toward the spot he showed her.

She missed his hands on her waist. She made to a secluded spot on shore and turned to speak to him.

She was alone.

She sat on the beach until she felt the familiar tingling and her legs reappeared. She scanned the faces of the swimmers in the ocean and waited, but she couldn't see Gareth.

So much for never letting her go.

He'd only meant while they were swimming through the dark water.

She was such a fool.

A teenager wearing a hotel T-shirt holding a stack of beach towels ogled her boobs. "The nude beach is that way, miss."

She tried to smile at him. Would she ever smile again? "Could I have one of those, please?"

"Yeah."

She took one and held it in front of her as she stood and wrapped it around her chest. Was her heart still beating?

She pulled herself out of her pity party. She had to think of her aunt and stop pining for somebody who only thought of her as a mission. A quick fuck, that was all he was.

Except he wasn't.

Would she ever see him again?

In a daze, she stole some clothes, flip flops, and pocket change left on empty lawn chairs on the beach and boarded a bus for the hospital, hoping to see her aunt before she went into surgery.

Aunt Cathy was talking to the anesthesiologist when Ainsley got there. Rob told her the doctors thought she needed a double bypass. Ainsley nodded as if it was news.

How could she explain she'd seen and heard them through the crystals?

They'd put her in the psych ward.

The anesthesiologist left them, and Ainsley hurried to her aunt's side.

Her aunt looked sickly pale. "You're back, sweetheart."

"I wanted to be here," she said.

Aunt Cathy eyes sparkled with mischief. "It's a fairly routine procedure these days. How was it, your father's hometown?"

"Unbelievable, Auntie."

Aunt Cathy squeezed her hand. "That dude who was hurt. Was he okay?"

Gareth. She couldn't think of him, not now.

Ainsley nodded. "I met my grandfather. He said my father died in the ocean trying to come back to Mom. He's all alone, his mate is dead, and they only had one child. But he's hundreds of years old. Things are different there."

"The man who was hurt. Tell me about him. He was sex on a stick."

Ainsley felt her cheeks flame. "I don't want to talk about him, Auntie, not right now."

"You came back, dearest girl," her aunt said.

Ainsley couldn't stop her tears. "He doesn't feel the same. He left me at the shore. But it's not important—you are."

Two orderlies, pushing a bed, appeared in the doorway.

"It's time," Rob said. He kissed her aunt on the lips passionately then broke away. "Love you," he said.

"Love you more," her aunt said.

Ainsley hugged her aunt. "Love you. See you later."

"Love you, too. Sometimes the best things, Ains, come when you stumble into them. Fight like hell to hold onto them. Don't be afraid to try."

The orderlies lifted her aunt onto the transport bed and wheeled her out.

She wagged her finger at them. "I'm a nurse, you know," she said.

Rob winked at Ainsley. "We are the worst patients. Come on, sugar. I'm starving."

❦

Lesia peered through the crystal. "She is taking food with a man in a shirt with flowers." She looked at Gareth. "She told him you didn't feel the same as she did, that you left her at the shore."

Cari, Rylan, their firstborn son, and Gareth's parents surrounded Lesia. Were there no secrets in the Crystal Caves?

"Why did you leave her?" Salina said. "We see how you look at her and how angry you get when you think that Micah will claim her."

He'd sent thoughts to Ainsley that he would never leave her when he felt her panic in the depths. He thought of the sapphires he wanted to fasten around her neck claiming her as his. He felt as if he left his life force with her. But she was where she wished to be. She had been relieved he hadn't planted his seed in her womb, hadn't she? Although he longed to see her belly swell with his offspring, repeatedly. "I tricked her to bring her back with me. She was a mission. I restored her to the place she wished to be, with her aunt."

"She weeps for wanting you," Cari said.

"What?" Gareth said. A kernel of hope bloomed.

"Her aunt is done with surgery." Cari smiled at their confusion. "The healers have finished their task.

Her aunt has told Ainsley to return to you, but she doesn't know how and believes you do not want her."

"Take our passes through the portal," Salina said.

Mature sea forms could only pass through the portal twice in an earth's revolution—unless they were on an ecommission—to ensure the ancient bridge through time and space did not become damaged through over-use. Gareth's parents used their passes to visit an island the land forms did not inhabit where coconuts grew. His mother loved to feast on the liquid and sweet white texture surrounding it.

Gareth bowed his head in thanks to his parents.

Cari, Rylan, and his parents chanted words of protection.

Gareth sheathed his knife and quartz crystal, made sure he had the necklace, and headed toward the portal.

Chapter 7

Swathed in sunscreen, Ainsley sat on a blanket at the nude beach where Gareth had left her. Rob and Aunt Cathy insisted she get out of the hospital. Aunt Cathy was going to be released tomorrow. Sara was getting Ainsley's mail, and she texted Ainsley, asking if she wanted her to open a letter from the school district.

~ *Yes*, Ainsley wrote.

~ *The letter says you're not getting tenure and are on probation for another year*, Sara replied.

~ *No surprise.*

Dickhead Packett put her on an action improvement

plan. If she didn't show noticeable improvement, she was out.

Fuck.

Rob had arranged for Aunt Cathy to recuperate at his friend's house on Oahu, where they'd scattered her mother's ashes. They were staying six weeks. Aunt Cathy was fretting about her condo on the Big Island so Ainsley was flying there tomorrow to stay in the house.

She stared at the surfers rather than at the vast ocean, and her panic stayed at bay. She emailed Sara.

~ *On nude beach. LOL.*

Sara answered back. ~ *GET LAID.*

Ainsley typed, ~ *Already did.*

~ *WTF. DEETS. GTG. LATER!!!* Sara answered.

Ainsley stretched out naked on top of the towel on the lounge chair she'd been lucky to find empty.

She'd shaved in the hotel room Rob booked for her, even her sex, which she loaded with sunscreen. She adjusted her sunglasses, shut her eyes, and nodded off.

Images of Gareth flitted through her dreams. She even heard him sing her name and felt his hands on her shoulders.

"Ainsley?"

She opened her eyes, and Gareth crouched next to her. She was dreaming. She shut her eyes.

He sat on the lounge chair and ran his hands over her suddenly heated skin. "No dream, Ainsley."

She licked her dry lips and he groaned. Again, she shut her eyes.

"I am dreaming about a shark fighter who left me here after he said he would never leave me."

His hands spanned her waist and he pressed his lips to hers. "No dream, Ainsley," he repeated.

He smelled like falling rain and tasted like Gareth. Her dreams didn't have smell or taste before.

He pulled her to her feet and into his arms. She went like a limp rag doll. "Ainsley, no more sun," he said. "Your skin will have damage." He looked around, scowled, then picked up the towel, and wrapped it around her, sarong style.

"It's a nude beach," she said. "I don't need this."

He gritted his teeth. "I do not wish other males to gaze at you."

He wore a loin cloth and a sheath. Most of the females on the beach couldn't take their eyes off him. "Every woman and girl here is ogling you," she said.

"We leave," he said.

"My clothes are in that bag." She pointed to a backpack.

Rob had given her his credit card, and she bought a T-shirt, shorts, and sandals in the hospital gift shop. "You have to wear something," she said.

She dropped the towel and pulled on her clothes while Gareth shielded her body.

A teenage guy holding a surf board walked past them and smirked. "Lighten up, dude. It's a nude beach."

Gareth growled in response and the kid scrambled away.

"Why are you here?" she asked.

He pulled her into his arms and kissed her again, slanting his mouth over hers. She kissed him back, and he deepened the kiss, exploring her mouth until she grew dizzy with wanting him. She lifted her mouth from his to breathe, and he pressed his face into her neck.

"Clothes, you need clothes," she said.

There was a gift shop on the roadway. Gareth stayed outside the store with the towel slung low on his hips. She grabbed some cargo shorts, flip flops, and a T-shirt.

Gareth put them on, and she drove Rob's rental SUV back to the motel by the hospital where Rob had booked her a room. She called her aunt in her hospital room. Aunt Cathy was sleepy so Ainsley said she'd see her tomorrow. She texted Rob that his SUV was at the motel.

Me too, he texted back.

He knocked on the door a couple minutes later and regarded Gareth, nodding curtly. Gareth nodded back.

Ainsley handed Rob the keys to his SUV. Rob squeezed her hand. "You okay, sugar?"

She nodded.

"I'm going to the hospital tomorrow morning at eight," Rob said.

Gareth put his hands on her shoulders.

"I'll be ready," she said.

Rob narrowed his eyes. "Call me if you need anything," he said, fishing his wallet out of his back pocket. He pulled out a credit card. "I put five hundred dollars on it."

He put it on the nightstand. She gave him back the credit card he'd given her earlier.

"Thanks," she said. "I'll pay you back, for this, the charges on the other card, and the cell phone."

Rob waved her off. With a hard look at Gareth, he said, "Later," then left them.

Gareth's hands left her shoulders, and he pushed her hair aside. He fastened a heavy necklace at her throat and heard it click shut. It was heavy, but it felt right, like it belonged there.

She went into the bathroom to look at it in the mirror. Huge blue stones sparkled like flame. "Sapphires?"

Gareth stood behind her. "Yes. Land forms call them this."

She gasped. It had to be priceless.

"Is first part of joining, if you wish it," he said. "Must be of your free will."

She stared into his eyes in the mirror. "What is joining besides…" Her voice trailed off.

His lips quirked into a smile. "If you wish to return to the Crystal Caves—we would be as Cari and Rylan. But I do not rule as Rylan."

She turned toward him and traced a scar on his bicep. "No, you are a shark fighter and restore ecosystems, the best at both, Ovon said. Why do you want a wife?"

He looked puzzled.

"Why do you want to join with me?"

He pulled her against him. "You weep for me."

He lifted her chin, and she looked into his green eyes streaked with gold. "My life force is not right without you," he said.

She kissed him then, pressing against him.

Could she leave everything and everybody she knew to be with him?

She felt a bond with Cari and Ovon in the Crystal Caves.

On land, she had Sara, her Aunt Cathy and Rob, and a handful of college friends she didn't see much anymore.

Gareth lifted her into his arms and spread her on the bed. He pulled off his shorts. His erection bulged through his loin cloth. He took off his shirt and his six-pack rippled. Did swimmers have six-packs?

She pulled her shirt over her head and slid out of her shorts. She didn't have time to buy underwear.

He stretched out on the bed and fingered her necklace. "I ache to be inside you." His green eyes were flecked with gold. He caressed the soft swell of her stomach. "You were relieved I did not plant my seed." He teased her nipples to stiff points. "Do you wish to join with me?" He moved his hand lower to her smooth sex. "This is different. You will stay like this when you learn your fins."

He bent his head and lapped at her sex with his tongue. She sunk her hands into his soft, sandy-colored hair. He sucked hard on her clit and she dissolved, screaming his name.

There was a knock on their door.

Holy hell.

Had they locked it?

She pulled the sheet up.

"You okay, Ains?"

It was Rob.

Fuck, fuck, fuck.

He heard her *three doors down*? "Yeah, sorry."

She got out of bed and latched the lock. Her cheeks flamed.

Gareth stood and took hold of her waist. He pressed kisses along her nape and put two fingers inside her wet slit.

"Do you wish it, Ainsley? You must say the words." He found her G-spot, and she would have sunk to the floor if he didn't have hold of her.

"Yes, darling, I want to join with you."

He pressed his thumb on her bundle of nerves, still sensitive, and she came again, turning her face into his shoulder to muffle her cries.

He laid her on the bed and thrust into her slick channel, stretching her and filling her. "Do you wish my seed?" He caressed her cheek.

She clenched her inner muscles around his thickness in response. "Yes, please."

He groaned. She writhed beneath him. "You wish to make your life with me under the waves?" He pumped into her, hitting all her nerve endings. She made a mewling noise. He stilled. "Ainsley?" His eyes searched hers, and he didn't breathe.

"Yes, shark fighter. I will go with you. But only if I will be the only female you join with. I know other females want to be with you after your fights. No groupies."

He scowled. "Groupies? You are only one I want."

He thrust hard, hitting the back of her womb. He kissed her then, his tongue mimicking his thrusts and she fell over the edge again, her cries muffled by his mouth.

They dozed before he took her again. She lay in his

arms, too shattered to move, when her stomach rumbled. "You have hunger," he said. He sat up, looking frustrated, and ran his fingers through his hair.

"There's a pizza place that delivers," she said.

"Do not move," he said.

She ogled his magnificent ass as he strode to the bathroom and returned with a damp washcloth. He pressed it between her legs then cleaned himself.

She reached for the menu from the pizza place Rob had left next to the motel phone and ordered Hawaiian pizza since she doubted anything else would compare with her favorite Detroit-style, deep-crust pizza with Italian sausage and olives she loved. She used the credit card Rob gave her to pay when she placed the order.

Micah had tried to explain how commerce worked in the Crystal Caves, but she couldn't follow his long-winded, detailed explanation.

Gareth pulled on his shorts and answered the door. He took the box but seemed puzzled with the two-liter bottle of Coke. She took two plastic glasses the motel provided and poured the Coke. "You have to try it. Most land forms like it, especially with pizza. Unless there's beer."

Did sea forms drink spirits? Or take drugs to get a buzz? Was that what shark fighting did for him? There was so much she didn't know.

He put the glasses on the nightstand then set the

pizza box on the bed. She remembered her mother feeding her apple slices and carrot sticks while they cuddled in her mother's bed.

He settled his long body on the bed with his back against the head rest and patted between his spread-out legs. "Here, darling." His grin reminded her of the first time she saw him. "Darling is word for person you join with. I hear Cari and Rylan."

She scrambled to sit between his legs. He eased her back against his chest, pulled the pizza box closer, took a slice out, held it to his lips for a moment, and then brought the corner to her lips.

She took a bite. The pineapple was not her usual topping of choice, but it wasn't bad.

She reached for a glass of coke. "Your turn."

He grunted. "It is murky and filled with land form chemicals. And this substance of this container makes problems for ecosystems."

"We'll recycle the plastic, there's a bin in the hospital. But you have to try one sip, it's to die for."

He tensed up, took the cup from her hand, and set it on the nightstand, spilling a bit on the floor. "No Ainsley." He cupped her chin, looking fierce. "You will not perish. I keep you safe."

He kissed her like he was starved for her. He released her and rested his forehead against hers. She turned in his arms and rested her cheek on his toned chest, over his thundering heart. "It's just an expression, something we say that means it tastes good. That's all."

She pulled away, took a sip from her glass, and kissed him so he could taste it.

"You taste best," he said.

He held the slice of pizza to her lips, and she devoured it. He reached for another, and she ate most of it, then waved him off. Only then did he eat. "Why did you feed me?" she said.

"We are joined, mostly," he said. "We speak final words in great hall."

"So those who are joined eat like this?" she said.

"And I wish it." His deep voice so close to her ear did funny things to her stomach and lady parts.

She had to focus. "I have so much to learn." She pulled out her cell phone and texted Sara, who, because of the time change, would be asleep.

~ *Plz take anything u want from my apt.* She had left her a key. *Lease up next mo. Married a guy who works offshore. Leaving asap. Emailing notice to Packett. Love u. Miss u. Hugs))*

She hit send and watched for a bit. No reply.

Good.

Gareth wiped tears from her cheeks. She didn't realize she'd been weeping.

"You love this Sara?" he said.

"We are teachers together at the place you first saw me. I'll miss her."

He took her phone from her and set it down then settled her on his lap on the only cushioned chair in the room. "We may come on land through the depths," he said.

The depths. Endless seas. She shivered. He sang her name in baritones until she calmed. "Or through the portal four times during an earth revolution, more times for ecommissions. Easiest to breach time and space through the portal during solstice and equinox. But you will not age as land forms. Sea forms in peril if discovered."

"Aunt Cathy and Rob know. My mother told them. Humans would think someone who talked about sea forms was ill, in their brain," she said.

But Sara would eventually notice and demand answers. He held her closer. "We visit your Sara for a time," he said. Had he read her thoughts?

"But we need money and clothes when we come on land. We'd need help with that," she said. Her aunt and Rob wouldn't be around forever. Rob had helped her so much when she returned. They would come on land as vagrants.

"There is lottery in some places," he said. "Sea forms can see some things, like outcomes, in crystals."

"We'd just need to steal money and clothes," she said. "And not win too much."

Had she been rash in deciding to follow him to a place alien to her? Could she overcome her fear of the open seas? She didn't want to live as her mother did, longing for someone she could never see or touch again.

No. She couldn't—wouldn't—walk away from Gareth.

He withdrew his arms and eased her off his lap then stood. He pulled a crystal from the sheath near his loin cloth, stared at it, and frowned. He paced and ran his fingers through his hair.

"Is something wrong?" she said.

He pulled on his shorts, shirt and slipped his wide feet into his flip-flops. "I go outdoors."

He unlatched the door. It snicked shut.

He would leave her in the Crystal Caves to restore habitat and fight sharks.

What would she do then?

What would she do in general?

She loved teaching and she was good at it, despite Packett's shitty review. Could she use her teaching skills in the Crystal Caves and find a place as Cari had done? Would the sea forms accept her?

Chapter 8

Gareth saw the quake rumble across the ocean floor in the crystal.

Would it reach the portal before he could bring Ainsley safely through? That was if she chose to leave land and say the final words to join them forever. They must leave soon.

Rob was also outside and came toward Gareth just as Ainsley stepped outside. "What's up?" Rob said.

Up? Gareth lifted his gaze.

Ainsley touched his arm. "It's an expression," she said. "It means what is happening or is something wrong?"

Gareth sighed. "Quake on bottom of sea heads toward portal."

"They'll need you to restore habitats that are damaged," she said.

"If you wish to return, we must leave soon," Gareth said.

"I wish it," she said.

"Say goodbye to your aunt," Rob said, pulling his car keys out of his pocket. "Come on."

Gareth sat in the front during the ride to the hospital. Music sounded from the device Ainsley used to send words to Sara. He swiveled in his seat as she pulled it out of her pocket.

"It's Sara." She pressed her finger on it then held it to her ear.

Sara's voice was such that Gareth could hear it. "What the fuck, Ainsley? Who texts that kind of message?"

"Things happened fast, Sar," Ainsley said. "And we have to leave soon."

"That's the point, Ains. Slow the fuck down. Are you sure about this dude? What's his name, for the love of God? What does offshore mean?"

"It's Gareth and he restores aquatic habitats all over the world," Ainsley said. "I'm going with him."

"You're afraid of water." Sara's voice was so loud

Ainsley pulled the device farther away from her ear. "You freaked out on Lake St. Clair."

"I love you, Sar. Be happy for me, please."

Rob stopped the vehicle in front of a large building.

"I'll text you my aunt's address if you want to ship anything, and my aunt will pay you back," Ainsley said. "Donate the furniture if you can't use it. It was my mother's and really old and not valuable. I'll email my resignation to Packett as soon as we hang up. We'll visit as soon as we can."

"I'll miss you so much," Sara said in resignation.

Tears coursed down Ainsley's cheeks. Gareth wanted to pull her into his arms.

"I'll miss you, too," Ainsley said. "Love you, Sar."

She slipped the device back in her pocket.

"You two go up," Rob said. "I'll park. Room two twenty-four."

Gareth got out, pulled Ainsley's door open, and took her into his arms.

She pressed her cheek into his chest for a moment, pulled away, and smiled up at him.

They walked inside. An older female sitting behind a table told them how to find Room two twenty-four.

Ainsley's aunt scowled when they entered her room. Another female slept in a bed next to her aunt. Ainsley pulled a curtain closed between them, kissed her aunt on her cheek, then put her arms around her, and wept.

"You don't have to do this, sweet girl," her aunt said.

Ainsley stepped back from her aunt and grabbed his hand. "And live my life with half a heart like Mom did?

"You were her heart," her aunt said.

"Oh, Auntie," Ainsley said, weeping.

He pulled her in, close to his body. How could he cause her such pain?

Her aunt jabbed her finger toward him. "You left her to fend for herself naked on that beach."

"I will not do so, never again," he said.

But as he said the words he knew he would have to leave her to restore habitats. And could he resist the call to fight sharks, even for his twin flame?

His crystal vibrated in his pocket, and he pulled it out. His sire sent a message to leave land soon if he meant to use the portal as they feared the quake could damage it.

"We must leave, darling," he said.

Ainsley embraced her aunt.

"When conditions are right, Cari talks with sibling on land and see each other's image," he said.

Ainsley let her aunt go and smiled at him. Her face was lit with joy.

He sucked in his breath, awed by her strength and beauty. Her auburn hair fell in soft waves to her shoulders, and her eyes rivaled the sapphires around her neck in color and luster.

"The necklace is beautiful," her aunt said.

"It signifies we have joined," he said.

Her aunt clasped Ainsley's hand. "Be happy, dearest girl, and bring her back if she isn't happy." She jabbed her finger toward him. He nodded.

Ainsley kissed her aunt. "I love you," she said.

"We go to the beach where I found you," he said.

"The nude beach," she said.

"Drive them, Rob," her aunt said. "I'll be here for hours, nobody's been in yet, and it's not that far."

"What is the address where you are staying, in case my friend needs to ship stuff?" Ainsley asked. "You could try to bill the cost to my credit card. I left it with my purse at your condo."

"No worries," Rob said.

She pulled out the device she called her cell phone and pressed her thumbs on it as Rob said numbers and words.

She continued to press her thumbs on it, scowling. "I'm emailing my resignation to my principal, the dick. He put me on probation because I told him I didn't want his son-in-law as my mentor, although I didn't know they were related. The creep kept hitting on me."

"This male hit you?" Gareth's urge for blood sport surged. "Are you hurt? When we next come on land, I will hunt him down and—"

She pressed her face to his neck. "No, darling, he did not hurt me. He wanted to have sex, join with me, although he was already joined with another."

Gareth did not understand many of the words she said to Rob and her aunt. It was frustrating to feel useless. He would do all he could to make Ainsley understand the ways and words in the Crystal Caves.

They left her aunt and got into Rob's vehicle. Gareth sat in the back with Ainsley so he could touch her skin and inhale her vanilla scent.

Rob stopped the vehicle next to other vehicles. Gareth opened the door. A crowd of land forms stood together on the smooth surface.

"One of the surfers is hurt, shark attack," a male said.

The color drained out of Ainsley's face.

"I'm an ER nurse," Rob said. "Can I help?"

"She's on the beach. We're waiting for nine-one-one," the same male said.

Rob ran to the beach.

Gareth felt for his knife, sheathed near his loin cloth. "How close?" he said.

"She paddled her board out and it took her arm," the male said.

Ainsley trembled. He took hold of her waist. "We cannot get to the portal until I…" He trailed off.

She swallowed hard. "Until you find it and kill it," she said.

He kissed her, tasting her as if was starved for her. "It will harm others," he said. "It has lost fear." All his needless shark fights had led him to this. "You must wait here. I will send word, as sea forms do."

She squared her shoulders and nodded. He sprinted toward the beach and veered away from the crowd. He took off his clothing and slipped unnoticed into the water.

The shark wasn't far from shore. His sea sight detected the dorsal fin. It was likely seeking more land-form prey.

Gareth unsheathed his knife and swam toward it. The shark detected him and turned its dead black eyes toward him.

He felt the familiar rush in his life force, but for the first time it was tempered with dead calm.

Never was so much at stake.

Never did he have so much to live for.

Half his life force waited for him on land.

The shark swam toward him. Unable to get a killing strike, he dodged, but too late. The shark clamped his jaws onto Gareth's tail fin, shredding it.

Gareth turned and plunged his knife though the shark's neck, killing it. Blood filled the water, and he wrenched his fin from the shark's jaws.

The healers could attend to his fin. But until they did, the injury would hamper his speed through the depths and weaken his life force. Ainsley would have to come to him in the sea.

He couldn't venture onto land in his injured state because he needed to conserve his strength. He tried to sync his thoughts to her, and sang her name in the way that seemed to soothe her.

'*Come to me, darling. I am in the sea, close to shore.*'

Did his words reach her? Could she conquer her fear of the vast sea to come to him and slip unnoticed through the throng of land forms?

∽∋∽∋

Gareth's voice sang her name and said to go into the water.

She headed for the beach, remembering the way his eyes blazed gold before he headed to the beach.

A policeman looked at her, frowning. "Stop, miss."

"My wallet, I left it. I'll just be a minute," she said.

The policeman's walkie-talkie crackled. She scrambled away from him toward the beach and stopped short at the sight of the endless sea. Her legs felt like sticks of wood.

He was waiting.

Could she do this?

She saw Rob tending to the wounded surfer.

Was Gareth hurt?

She ran to the water's edge. "Miss, stop," a man called out.

She shut her eyes against the vast expanse of water and swam out as far as she could, slipping out of her shorts in case she took her sea form.

Where was he?

The farther out she swam, the darker the water became. She had to surface to drag air into her lungs.

"Suicide, she's trying to kill herself," someone said.

She submerged, and Gareth's voice synced into her head.

'Here, darling.'

'Where?'

She propelled herself into the open sea as far as she could when she felt a wave coming. It would push her back to shore.

She heard the whir of an engine, a rescue boat? Giving it everything she had, ignoring her lungs demand for air, she struck out for the bottom, fighting panic and dread that she would never see him again.

❧❦❧

His heart felt as if it would explode as he pulled her down to the ocean floor. A motor whirred above them. He fused his mouth to hers, infusing her with his life force as he shifted her to her sea form.

His clever female had shed her garment that would have hampered that.

'*Gareth?*'

His name pierced through his soul.

'*Are you hurt?*' she asked.

'*Yes. Only my tail.*'

A land form wearing devices that allowed him to breathe and move underwater swam above them, shining a light. They made their way to the portal as the light came closer. They entered the portal, and he held her tight as they went through the vortex, bridging time and space.

They came to a halt in a cave under the waves, sealed off from the riptides where he could subsist on the essence of pure water, and Ainsley would have the air her land form lungs still needed.

What was this place? There was an ancient legend of such a place where newly joined sea forms journeyed, but none of those who lived in the Alliance cities had ever seen it. The walls glittered with veins of multi-colored crystal.

Abundant sea forms they could eat inhabited the shallow pools in the cavern. He pulled her, then himself, out of the water, wincing as his injured tail scraped against the ledge. He held her against him and sang her name.

"Your tail," she said.

"The healers will care for it," he said. "It is a common injury."

He mulled over the shark fight. He had never misjudged his form in proximity to a shark's before. He was not wholly focused on the battle. He would never be again.

He would think of Ainsley before all things.

He was done shark fighting.

She had braved the sea that filled her with fear to come to him.

He'd found something that he'd never dreamed existed for him, his twin flame.

Shark fighting was nothing to that.

As they took their land forms, a gash appeared on his leg. Blood seeped from the wound.

She gasped, took off the clothing that covered her breasts, and pressed it to his leg. "To stem the flow. My mom was a nurse like Rob and Aunt Cathy."

He palmed her breasts as she bent toward him. "I like you this way best, when no other males can see you."

She left the cloth in place, sticking to his leg, and looked around the grotto. "What is this place? Is it part of the Crystal Caves?"

"No," he said.

He pulled the crystal from his sheath and stared into it.

His sire came into focus. "The portal is damaged," Endon said. "Are you safe?"

"I think we are in the grotto the ancients spoke of," Gareth said in the language of the Crystal Caves. "My tail is injured."

Endon looked angry. "Shark fight?"

"The shark injured a land form close to the shore we had to swim from to reach the portal."

"It will be seven earth rotations before the portal is restored," Endon said.

"There is abundant food," Gareth said.

"Lesia said the mineral pools said to be there would help you heal and there should be a spot to a...rest." His sire smiled.

"We will speak the final words to join when we return," Gareth said.

His mother's smiling image replaced his sire's. "Take great care. We await your return."

She chanted words of protection, and he bowed his head to receive them.

The chant faded, and he stood, sheathed the crystal,

and took Ainsley in his arms. "We stay here seven earth rotations until portal is restored. Lesia says there should be mineral pools to heal the wound."

The gash throbbed when he moved his leg. He sucked in a breath.

"I'll go," she said. "You stay here."

He took firm hold of her waist. "No, we will not part," he said.

They made their way to the far end of the grotto where green vines clung to a damp wall next to a green, shallow pool uninhabited by sea forms. He left her garment sticking to his leg, sat near the edge, and lowered it into the water.

The pain ebbed.

"It's green," she said, sitting next to him.

"The pain is ending," he said.

She wrapped her arms around his waist and rested her cheek against his back. "How is it this place has light?"

"Energy from crystals," he said, breathing in her scent. "My sire says there may be a place here to rest in comfort."

"I can't see any place like that from here," she said.

He scanned the walls for passages and saw nothing.

She squeezed his arm. "That could be it," she said. "Look down." She stood and took a couple steps away from him then pointed. "Along that channel. There's an incline near another small green pond with long blades of something on the flat part." She shivered. "I hope they're not alive. It looks like grass but it's white."

He lifted his leg out of the water.

She gasped. "Your wound. I can barely see it."

"I do not feel pain," he said.

She smiled. "So you can still fight sharks."

He took her hand and led her to the spot she'd found where the white blades grew. "They are as grass on land. And, no, I cannot fight sharks. I erred because of you."

❧❧❧

He sounded angry.

She flinched. Hell no. Shark fighting was part of who he was.

He turned away from her and inspected what looked like tiny berries growing on a vine spouting up from the channel. They were white like the grass.

Oblivious to her anger, he picked a berry, held it on his tongue, and then took a small bite. He turned back to her. "Do you feel hunger? This has sweetness and will not harm us."

Her stomach felt like it was filled with cement. "Not now. Why can't you fight sharks? You said it was because of me, and I don't understand. I am not asking you to give it up."

He drew her down on the soft white blades. They felt dry and squishy. She sat stiff against him.

"You fill my thoughts," he said. "For shark fights, you must think only of that."

"No," she said. He would grow to hate her for being the reason he stopped doing what he loved. "I won't join with you if you stop shark fighting. Take me back to land when it's safe."

She scrambled away from him.

ೞೞೞ

He let her go because he could reach her quickly if he had to.

Was she like those females who clamored for attentions of those who bested sharks? He pushed that thought aside and focused on reading her thoughts. He felt her fear that he would hate her and blame her for ruining his shark fighting skill.

The blood sport energized his life force, but she *was* his life force. He'd felt her fear for him when he'd left her to battle the shark that attacked the land form. He knew she would feel fear when he left her in the Crystal Caves to restore ecosystems. But he would not cause her distress over needless shark fighting.

He had seven earth rotations to convince her that his need for her eclipsed all things. He ate the berries that drew nutrients for sustenance from the mineral water and put his leg in the pool so it would grow stronger. He longed to go to Ainsley and make her understand it was she who sustained his life force, not shark fighting, but he forced himself to stay still and think.

He would need to draw upon all his skill and focus he used restoring habitats and shark fighting for the fight of his life—to win Ainsley, heart, body, and soul.

Chapter 9

Ainsley ran her finger along what looked like a vein of gold in the wall of the cavern. She could find another job.

She hadn't been insulting or rude in her resignation email. Maybe she could stay in Hawaii to live close to her aunt.

Sara could visit.

She ignored the thought that she would be the shell her mother was without Gareth. She loved him so much. That's why she had to let him go.

She felt him near her. She couldn't face him, not yet. She couldn't let him see how hard this was for her or how much she wanted him. "How do things grow here?" she said.

He lifted her hair off her neck and pressed his lips to her nape. "On land you say hydroponics," he said. "Light reflects from crystals."

"Oh, the minerals in the water," she said.

His hand pressed into her belly and, against her resolve, she melted against him.

"You must take food and rest," he said, lifting her into his arms.

He strode to the spot where the pale grass grew and set her down next to the small pond.

He followed her down and settled her between his legs, her back to his chest, and fed her the white, sweet things that looked like pearls growing on the vine.

His hand strayed to her necklace, then her nipples, brushing over them till they were stiff and aching for his touch.

"My shirt," she said. "Where is it?"

He pointed to a sodden heap on the pathway. His arm brushed her breast, sending tremors to her core. He groaned against her neck, and his other hand cupped her sex.

He slid two fingers inside her slick channel, and she was lost.

His finger found her G-spot and she saw stars, screaming her release.

When she opened her eyes, she was on her back, his erection rubbed against her folds. His eyes blazed gold. "Do you wish this?" he said.

She loved him so much. All she could do was nod. He plunged into her, murmuring words she couldn't understand as his eyes raked over her. He wrapped her legs around his waist so he could thrust even deeper. He tweaked her nipples and she came in a warm gush. She shut her eyes.

He nipped her lower lip. "Look at me, darling. It is the same for me. I would be this shell you think of without you."

Shell? He picked up her thoughts of her mother. He pumped into her, and she came again when he emptied himself inside her. He made no move to pull out, but rolled so they were on their sides. She pressed her cheek to his chest and heard his heart beat.

"You are my heart. We are twin flames." he said, as she shut her eyes and went to sleep.

She woke up alone in the odd white grass. He was using her shirt as a fish net to scoop fish from the waters. He used his knife to fillet them then aimed his crystal at the veins of blue threaded in the walls of the cavern and flash-cooked the fish. He fed her first then ate the rest.

They drank from a trickle of fresh water in a wall of rock threaded with amethyst.

Every time she steeled her resolve to leave him, he made love to her until she came, screaming his name. She didn't know how long they had been there. It was always light.

He pulled out his crystal and spoke with his father, nodded, then sheathed it. He put his hands on her shoulders.

A nerve in his cheek twitched. "It is time. The portal is restored. Will you return with me and speak final joining words?"

Her heart hurt and she shook her head. "You are a shark fighter. I saw your face before you left to do battle. You looked so masterful—in command. Nobody said anything to stop you, when you went onto the beach, did they?"

"No," he said.

"The police gave me a hard time," she said.

His grip on her shoulders tightened. "You were hurt?"

"No," she said. "They wanted me to be safe. They didn't want me to go on the beach. I had to tell them a lie so they would let me go. You were meant to fight sharks, take command. It's your destiny. I can't—I won't ruin that for you."

His touch on her shoulders softened. "You are my destiny. I very much like commanding your body when we join. You are mine."

Tears coursed down her cheeks. "What if you must do it again, and you can't because of me? It's not fair to you," she said, remembering her Packett's shitty evaluation. "Someone was unfair to me and tried to stop me from teaching children, something I love and I'm good at. I can't do that to someone I love."

☙❧☙❧

She loved him.

She'd never said the word before. He shut his eyes and savored her words. They counted as free will. She belonged to him. And he belonged to her. The rest was a misunderstanding. He would not let her go.

He chanted words of forgiveness for what he would do.

He led her to the spot Endon where described. "We leave now," he said. "I will take you where you wish."

She picked up her shirt. "I'll need this," she said.

Except she wouldn't.

"I love you, Ainsley," he said, before he crushed her mouth under his.

They propelled through the vortex.

☙❧☙❧

The Crystal Caves.

She recognized the formations. "You tricked me," she said.

He slipped white robes left near the entrance to the portal over their heads.

"You said you'd take me where I wished."

She slipped her arms through the gown and he adjusted her necklace over the modest neckline of the silky fabric.

"You spoke words of love to me. Means you wish to be here, with me." He took hold of her waist. "We speak final words to join in the great hall."

She put her hand on his chest. "You cheated. I said I wanted to go back to land."

He pulled her closer. His erection nudged against her. "Yes, I pressed my advantage. You belong here with me. I restore habitats. This is your true place."

"I must say the final words by my own free will, right?" She pulled away from him so she could read his expression. "You could get in trouble, again, if I say you tricked me."

His lips quirked into a smile. "I care not."

"Gareth? Ainsley?" Salina and Endon called out and came toward them. They bowed their heads and chanted.

Gareth drew her to his side.

"All await in the great hall," Salina said, smiling.

Gareth and his father spoke in the language of the

Crystal Caves. Gareth let Ainsley go as they walked along the channel.

Salina walked beside her and asked about the grotto.

"The mineral pools were amazing," Ainsley said. "Gareth was hurt but he healed."

"You are distressed, Salina said.

"He says he will not fight sharks because I distract him," Ainsley said.

Salina looked confused.

"He says he cannot focus on the shark because he thinks of me."

Salina bowed her head and chanted. "I am happy for that. But this is your distress."

"He loves it, and I can't be the reason he stops," Ainsley said.

"It was pointless folly," Salina said. "He is skilled beyond all others at restoring balance to damaged habitat. That and you are his destiny." Salina touched her arm. "He waited for you though he didn't know this. He is too stubborn to look in the hall of records or through the crystals."

They rounded a corner and formations like chandeliers hung from the high ceiling in what had to be the great hall. Salina drew her onto a cushioned bench and shooed Gareth and his father away.

Two young female sea forms worked through the

tangles in Ainsley's hair and arranged it in an updo threaded with tiny pale blue gems. Then they rubbed light fragrant oil on her skin.

Giggling, the young females smoothed balm on her lips and lined her eyes with reeds dipped in a dark powder.

When they were finished, Salina motioned for her to stand and tied a purple sash with threads of gold around her waist.

Sea forms began to assemble. Ainsley looked at their faces. Some were smiling shyly, some held no expression, and some looked at her in distaste.

It reminded her of the kid's faces on the first day of school.

"Ainsley?" Cari touched her shoulder. She wore her hair in a thick braid threaded with red gemstones that hung over her shoulder and a gown of the same purple fabric as Ainsley's sash. Her stomach bulge was noticeably larger.

Rylan stood behind Cari. His hands caressed her shoulders.

Cari patted her bulge and smiled. "Gestation is faster in the depths but children age as they do on land. The aging process slows down in adulthood." She glanced around the room at the staring faces. "You will earn their trust in time," she said.

Gareth stood near a raised platform. Rylan kissed Cari's nape then left to take a seat on the platform, next to Lesia and others.

Ovon came toward her, beaming. He looked resplendent in a red robe.

Ainsley squeezed both his hands. "Grandfather."

Cari said a word she didn't understand and Ovon bowed his head and chanted. A murmur went through the crowd.

"I explained what grandfather means to the rest of the sea forms," Cari said. "This has pleased them."

Ovon offered Ainsley his arm, and they walked toward the platform were Gareth waited. Cari walked behind them. Ainsley shook with nerves. Ovon bowed to her, stepped back, and Gareth took hold of her cold hands.

A woman with long, white hair, unlined face, wearing a gold robe, stood on the platform. Gareth spoke words Ainsley didn't understand. The crowd gasped.

Cari translated. "He said you wished to return to land, not here, with him. That you are upset he won't fight sharks because of his love for you. He said he believes you love him but do not want to be the reason he stops. He loves you beyond all else and realizes shark fighting is wrong and against the principles of dominion and stewardship for sea forms those in the Alliance Cities hold sacred."

"Holy hell," Ainsley said. "What do I say now?"

Gareth's watched her intently. A nerve twitched in his cheek.

"Forever, it is done," Cari whispered. "Those are the final joining words."

Ainsley squeezed Gareth's hands. "What happens to you if I don't say those words?"

Cari started to speak.

"No," Gareth said. "I do not want her to know this."

He said other words she didn't understand and another gasp went through the crowd.

"He has said he told you he does not care what happens to him if you refuse," Cari said, touching her arm. "He truly doesn't. He's crazy for you, Ainsley."

His eyes took on the gold cast she understood meant he was in throes of passion or battle, like they did before he left her to battle the shark at the nude beach. He was fighting, she realized, fighting for her.

The last bit of doubt melted away. She thought of the vast ocean above them and shivered. But she would fight that fear, as he was fighting for her.

She leaned down and pressed her lips to both of his hands, nicked with scars from shark fighting and his work restoring ecosystems, and restoring her.

"I love you," She smiled. "Forever, it is done."

He let go of her hands, took hold of her waist, lifted her, and spun her around, laughing joyfully. "Forever, it is done." His voice thundered through the room.

The applause was deafening as he lowered her against him and fused his mouth to hers. She kissed him back, trying to show him how much she loved him, not caring they stood in a hall with hundreds of sea forms watching.

He broke off the kiss, lifted her in his arms, and carried her along a series of passageways to his chamber.

"Our chamber, darling," he said. An array of every type of sea food, and other things she couldn't name was spread out with goblets filled with amber liquid on a long shelf.

"Our wedding feast," she said.

He put her down, undid her sash and pulled her gown off over her head, then pulled his off. "I like you best this way," he said. His erection strained against his loin cloth.

But first she had to know what would have happened to him if she had rejected him. She took hold of his hands and sank to her knees. "Gareth, I have to know. What would have happened to you if I demanded you take me to land? I want us to start with a clean slate."

He looked confused. "There is no slate in this part of the Crystal Caves."

Damn. She had to stop using expressions that confused him. She taught third graders. She could do this. "No secrets, only truth for us," she said. "Please, darling."

He pulled her up firmly against him so the top of her head was tucked under his chin. He sighed. "I would be given tasks assigned to sea forms still learning their fins, not permitted to assist on ecomissions and take orders from Micah."

She pulled away from him and gripped his shoulders. "That's like prison without bars."

Her legs felt like jelly. He lifted her onto the bed then loaded a large, flat shell with morsels of food, set it next to the bed, and arranged his long, lean body so she was settled between his legs. She rested her head back on his shoulder.

He fed her morsel after morsel of succulent lobster, shrimp, and crab in between bites crispy vegetables and sweet citrusy berries. She sucked his fingers clean between bites and wiggled her backside against his erection.

When she couldn't take another bite, she batted his hand away. "I want dessert."

She scooted down, freed his bulging erection from his loin cloth, and licked off the pre-cum from the tip before she sucked his tip in earnest, cupping his balls.

He moaned and pulled her away from him. "My turn."

Before she could protest, he spread her legs and lapped her sex. He slid two fingers inside her wet slit and she came instantly, screaming his name.

Would it always be like this?

She remembered Rob pounding on their motel room door when she screamed her release and giggled.

Gareth watched her, tracing lazy circles around her nipples.

"I love your laughing, but why?" He pinched her nipples, which made her wetter.

"Rob heard me screaming in the motel room and banged on the door, thinking something was wrong..." Her voice trailed off as waves of embarrassment coursed through her. What if the sea forms heard her? "Shit, oh shit, oh shit."

He cupped her face. His eyes filled with concern. "What is your distress?"

"What if someone heard me?"

He laughed. "Our chamber is far from others, and we are newly joined. It is expected."

He nudged her sex with his rock hard cock. "But it will be like this for us always, I think. It is the way with twin flames."

"Really? On land when people age, their sex drives

fade." He teased her sensitive bundle of nerves with his erection. She moaned. She was insatiable.

"My sire and mother's want hasn't faded. I hear them, so I am here, also far from my sibling and her twin flame. They are on ecommission. My mother and sire watch over their offspring. They clamor to meet you."

He thrust into her bottoming out in her womb. She clenched her muscles around him.

He groaned and chanted words in the language of the Crystal Caves. "You send me to where land forms call heaven," he said. He pulled out, hitting every nerve ending.

He was a skilled and generous lover. He must have pleased many females. She remembered his cocky swagger the first time she met him, and he smirked at her poster of *Shark Week*.

How could she stack up against all his groupies?

He stared into her eyes, stilled and pulled on her necklace.

Had he read her thoughts?

"I cared not for any female," he said. "I know that is bad. Only you, Ainsley. I had to claim you. I did not have that need for any female, ever."

His eyes blazed gold and his cheek twitched, his tells he was distressed. Her jealousy faded and she longed to reassure him. She put her hand over his beautiful mouth.

"I hate the thought that you touched other females," she said. "It makes me crazy jealous, like you were when I brought that guy home from the bar when you first came on land."

He growled and thrust into her.

"You read my thoughts, but I don't know yours, not right now," she said. She caressed his jaw.

He bit down on the fleshy part of her palm. "Sea forms must do this in the depths to stay safe. You will always read my thoughts also, with practicing." He smiled. "Try."

She stared into the green depths of his eyes and it was like a bubble burst in her brain. Babies, he wanted to give her babies and see her body swell with the life he put inside her.

"I want that, too," she said. "And to help with your work and teach children English and learn your language—"

His mouth crashed down on hers in a hard, possessive kiss as he pounded another orgasm from her then poured his seed into her womb. He collapsed on top of her and she held him fiercely.

He pressed his lips to her ear. "You will do all these things you wish," he said. "For as long as I draw breath, I will love you and see you happy. Forever, it is done."

And it was.

THE END

About the Author

Tara Eldana is an award-winning staff writer for a weekly community newspaper chain in metro Detroit. She became hooked on romance fiction when her eleventh grade English teacher rejected the book report she wrote, saying the book was much too easy for her, and insisted she read and report on Daphne du Maurier's *Rebecca*. Eldana had read Margaret Mitchell's *Gone With the Wind* that previous summer.

Eldana took a long road through J-school, graduating from Oakland University in Rochester, Michigan in '95.

She loves the romance genre and loves letting her characters take control of their stories. Eldana is a member of the Greater Detroit Romance Writers of America.

Connect with her on Facebook, Twitter, or visit her website at taraeldana.com.